SHADOWS
ON THE SEA

ALSO BY JOAN HIATT HARLOW

Star in the Storm
Joshua's Song

SHADOWS
ON THE SEA

Joan Hiatt Harlow

SCHOLASTIC INC.

New York Toronto London Auckland Sydney
Mexico City New Delhi Hong Kong Buenos Aires

In loving memory of my dad,
Albert E. Hiatt,
who filled my life with song!

CONTENTS

SHADOWS
ON THE SEA

1

Jill's Transformation

Don't worry so much! Don't worry so much!

Jill Winters leaned her forehead against the train window and peered out through the raindrops at the early summer landscape. It was bleak—more like April than June. At another time the sound of the wheels clicking over the tracks might have lulled her to sleep. But today it mingled with the thoughts and regrets that pounded in her head.

Don't worry so much! Don't worry so much!

Earlier this month, her father, a popular singer, flew out to California to do some concerts and radio shows. It was nice to have a famous father, but Jill missed him when he traveled. Even though the country was at war, Dad's popularity had snow-balled—not only because of his beautiful voice and good looks, but because he touched the hearts of his audiences with his stage presence and down-to-earth charm. His agent was booking him for appearances here, there, and just about everywhere.

Less than a week after Dad left, Mom had gotten the news that her brother, Jill's uncle Cliff, was critically ill with cancer. Mom was determined to go to the British colony of Newfoundland to take care of him. "I'll be all right, Jill," her mother assured her. "I'll be taking the *Caribou* across the Gulf of St. Lawrence. It's just a merchant ship. It won't be a target for German submarines." But everyone knew Newfoundland was an important military base for American and Canadian troops. U-boats—German submarines—patrolled the waters around the great rocky island like circling sharks waiting . . . waiting.

Jill's mother's amber eyes filled with tears when Jill had begged, "Let me go with you!"

"I can't take you, darling. The only reason

they're letting me go is that I'm next of kin to Cliff—and a registered nurse. They won't let me take a child along. It may be dangerous."

"I'm *not* a child. I'm fourteen. Besides, if it's too dangerous for *me*, it's too dangerous for *you!*" Jill argued.

"Jill, I've *got* to go," Mom explained. "Cliff is in a far-off port and he's all alone. He needs me."

"*I* need you!"

"Jill, he's my brother!" Mom had said impatiently. "You can't understand, because you don't have brothers or sisters."

"You care more about Uncle Cliff than *me*! I'll bet Daddy will let me join him in California, if I ask him!" Jill stomped off to her room, threw herself on her bed, and hugged her pillow.

Her father had called that night but spoke to Mom first. When Jill took the telephone in her room, she waited until her mother hung up the extension, then pleaded, "Can I come out to California, Daddy?"

But Dad said, "No, Jill. It's not safe for you to be traveling all over the country on a crazy schedule like mine." There was a long silence, then he said, "You know, Nana would love to have you spend some time with her in Maine this summer."

Her father hung up and, within a few minutes, called back. "It's all set. Nana is tickled to pieces to have you stay with her."

Summer in Maine? It sounded awful. Even though she loved Nana, Jill didn't want to go. She didn't have any friends up there—she'd be bored and lonely all summer.

When Mom left a few days later, she tried to give Jill a hug, but Jill pulled away. Before getting into the taxi, her mother threw a kiss to Jill, who watched from the window. Jill grudgingly nodded good-bye but didn't send a kiss.

Jill's best friend, Patty, and her mother, Mrs. Hayden, had come to stay with Jill until she left for Maine the following week. "You should have been kinder to your mother, Jill. She's going on a sad mission." Mrs. Hayden frowned her disapproval. "Besides, we're at war and everyone has to make sacrifices. Your mother had to make a hard choice and you didn't make it any easier for her."

Jill slumped on the couch, guilty and scared. What if something happened to Mom? Jill wished she had thrown that good-bye kiss. She got up and ran to the window but the taxi was gone. Jill's eyes brimmed and she reached for one of her mother's lace-trimmed handkerchiefs that was left crumpled on the coffee table. As Jill wiped her eyes she could smell the scent of Tweed, her mother's favorite perfume. She choked back a sob.

After her mother left, Jill began paying more attention to radio news. She heard Walter Winchell report that from January to June this very year—1942—more than 170 ships had been sunk in American waters. Innocent American, Canadian, and Newfoundland merchant vessels— like the *Caribou*—silhouetted against brightly lit East Coast cities, were easy targets for the German U-boats.

Today Patty and her mother had driven Jill to Boston to take the train to Maine. "Lucky you, traveling all the way to Winter Haven alone! It's so . . . mature." Patty kissed her good-bye, then whispered, "Have fun! Once the train starts, get into those glamorous slacks and pretend you're sixteen."

Patty was right, Jill decided. Taking a train by

herself really *was* mature. Her folks felt she was mature enough to travel all the way up the coast by herself. She'd get along just fine without her parents. She didn't need them one single bit. Yet, she couldn't forget how sad Mom had looked when she said good-bye.

Jill looked at her reflection in the train window. There she was. Jill Elizabeth Winters. Her brown hair hung to her shoulders in natural curls. Her eyes were large, wide-set, and the color of honey. In the reflection, her face stood out rather pale against the white Peter Pan collar on her dress. I hate Peter Pan collars, she thought. They are so childish!

Patty had said, "Have fun." Well, if she had to be on this miserable trip, she'd make the most of it. After all, she was on her own for the first time. She'd try to stop worrying so much and do whatever she felt like doing. And right now she felt like getting rid of that Peter Pan collar!

Jill pulled out the smaller of her two suitcases from under the seat, then headed for the lavatory at the far end of the passenger car. Once inside, she locked the door and put her bag on the floor. She peered into the toilet and could see the train tracks and crossties zooming by. That's awful! she thought. The toilets don't flush—they just empty out onto the ground!

She slammed the cover down, sat on the seat, opened her bag, and took out her new slacks. Grinning, she held them up. A nice shade of blue cotton sateen. Her parents would die if they knew how she'd spent her clothing money. Slacks had become more acceptable since the war had started, especially for women working in factories where skirts could be dangerous. Movie stars were beginning to wear them everywhere. However, girls were not allowed to wear slacks to school. When Jill begged for a pair, Mom had said, "Overalls are okay for a hike in the woods, but slacks for everyday use are just not ladylike."

Patty's mom let the girls have a special day together after Jill's mother had left. Jill secretly bought the slacks suit. Patty giggled and swore she'd never tell. Jill wasn't sure what Nana's reaction would be. I can handle Nana, she told herself confidently.

Jill removed her dress and scowled at it. So prissy and juvenile! After taking off her slip, she pulled on the slacks, donned a flowered blue-and-tan shirt, and peered into the small mirror over the sink. She braided her hair, weaving a blue grosgrain ribbon into the thick braid. That looks glamorous, she thought, just like Dorothy Lamour in the movie *Road to Singapore*. Finally she slipped into the matching jacket. It had huge shoulder pads in the newest military style.

Jill fumbled through her bag until she found her white bobby socks. Hidden in one was a tube of Tangee lipstick. Her parents had made it clear she couldn't wear lipstick until she was sixteen. Carefully she applied the Tangee and pressed her lips together. It was such a pale orange it could hardly be noticed, so she applied it again. When she got to Maine, she'd buy some real lipstick.

Jill jumped up and down, straining to see her whole image in the small mirror. That's better! I really *do* look sixteen, she decided with a smug grin. She stuffed her dress and slip into her bag and snapped it shut.

Satisfied and feeling quite mature, Jill stepped out of the rest room just in time to hear the porter call out, "Supper is being served in the dining car."

2

Scarlett

Although it was wartime, the dining car maintained a sense of elegance. Little battery-operated lamps flickered on tables, which were covered with starched white tablecloths and linen napkins. Jill was escorted to a table by a smartly dressed waiter who handed her a menu. A small notice on the menu explained how the Boston & Maine Railroad was attempting to keep the selections varied despite war-rationing restrictions. The meal was paid for in the price of her ticket, so Jill could have whatever she chose.

"I'll have a hot turkey sandwich and a pot of

tea, please," she told the waiter. Her mother, a Newfoundlander and therefore a British subject, had been brought up with the English custom of having tea every afternoon. There was something about a cup of tea that made Jill feel comfortable and grown-up.

While she waited for her order, she gazed around the dining car. Two sailors were joking and laughing at a table in the corner. Across the aisle, a dark-haired gentleman sipped wine and studied the menu.

A blast of wind caught Jill's attention as someone opened the door and entered the car. A girl who appeared to be a little older than Jill sauntered down the aisle.

She wore a gray dress with a draped bodice and flared skirt, but the wide black diagonal stripes were eye-catching. Her blond hair was smoothly turned into a stylish pageboy and curved prettily at her cheeks. To top it off, this girl was wearing *silk* stockings! Jill could tell they were silk—so sheer and smooth. Where did she *ever* get silk stockings with the war going on?

Jill found herself staring, and as the girl

turned, looking for a table, their eyes met. Embarrassed, Jill looked quickly down at her hands.

The girl stepped over to Jill's table. "Is anyone sitting with you? Would you like some company?" She smiled, one dimple appearing on her right cheek.

Jill shrugged and nodded.

The newcomer slid into the opposite seat. "I'm on my way to the shore for the summer. I'm from New York. I find the heat in the city quite oppressive, don't you?"

"I don't live *in* the city," Jill answered. "I live *outside* Boston."

"Oh, you're a country girl then?" The stranger removed her white gloves and placed them neatly by her plate.

"No, I'm not a country girl," Jill blurted. Did she *look* like a country girl in her slacks and Dorothy Lamour hairdo?

The girl seemed engrossed in the menu. She then gave her order to the waiter who hovered over her, filling her water glass and adjusting the silverware. Jill peered a little closer. Yes, she was wearing a touch of red lipstick—it was *not* Tangee.

After the stranger ordered a cup of tea and a plate of finger sandwiches, she settled back in her seat and looked out the window. "I hate traveling backward."

Jill was *not* about to switch seats.

"Oh, my name is Scarlett," the girl continued. "Like in the movie, *Gone With the Wind.* Everyone comments on my name. Only *my* name's Scarlett Jones—not O'Hara."

"I'm Jill Winters."

"Where are you going, if you don't mind my asking?"

"To the shore," Jill answered. "I'm spending the summer at my grandmother's estate. She owns a gorgeous home by the sea." Jill had never been to Nana's house. Nana had purchased it a few years ago, after Grandfather died. From photographs, Nana's house looked old and comfortable, with a big porch overlooking the ocean. However, it was weather-beaten and certainly *not* gorgeous. But this girl would never know.

"How nice. I'll be managing a tearoom and

inn. It's hard to find help with the war on, you know. I'm doing it as a favor to my aunt. She's begged me to come and help her out. I know a lot about publicity and things, since my father is a producer in the film industry."

"He is? What film company?"

"Metro-Goldwyn-Mayer, Twentieth Century Fox—all the big ones."

"I'll watch for his name on the film credits," Jill said.

"Maybe you'll see it. Maybe not. They scroll the names very quickly." Scarlett smoothed her hair. "Daddy has promised to get me an ingenue lead in one of his movies very soon. I study drama at school."

Ingenue? Some theatrical term, I suppose, Jill thought, feeling stupid.

"Daddy thinks I need a little change away from the theater, so he decided I should come to Maine for the summer. It will also give me a taste of seaside living, since that will be the background of his new movie."

The waiter served their dinners together and both girls were quiet as they ate.

Out of the corner of her eye, Jill watched Scarlett admiringly. She poured tea from the silver-plated teapot with her little finger pointed straight out. Using tongs, she delicately dropped tiny squares of sugar into her cup. "Sugar?" she asked Jill. "Cream?"

"No, thank you." Jill tried cutting her turkey sandwich into smaller pieces, holding *her* little finger out in the same elegant manner, but it felt awkward and she couldn't get a good grip on her knife.

When they were finished, Scarlett patted her lips, then set the napkin on the table. "Now, Jill, tell me about your family."

"My father is a singer. Maybe you've heard of him. Drew Winters?"

Scarlett's blue eyes widened. "Drew Winters is *your* father?"

"Yes. He's performing in California right now. My mother is traveling . . . overseas."

"Overseas? With the war going on?"

"I'm awfully worried about her," Jill said truthfully.

Scarlett looked skeptical.

She doesn't believe me, Jill thought. Well, I

can make this more interesting. "Actually, my mother works for intelligence. She's a spy."

Scarlett looked suspiciously at Jill. "If your mother was really a spy, you wouldn't be telling anyone."

Jill cleared her throat and lowered her voice. "You're right. Of course, I shouldn't be talking about my mother. I have to be careful. The war, you know." She glanced quickly around and gestured to a poster on the wall that showed the figure of Uncle Sam with a finger to his lips and the words *Loose lips sink ships*.

For a while neither girl spoke. Then Scarlett said, "So your father is Drew Winters and your mother is a spy."

Suddenly Jill had no idea what she could possibly say next. Her problem was solved as the conductor walked through the dining car. "We will be arriving in Bangor in five minutes," he announced.

Jill got up. "Nice meeting you, Scarlett. Have a good summer." She didn't linger for Scarlett to say good-bye but raced back the length of two cars to her own seat. Then, gathering her luggage together, she waited for the train to stop.

"Bangor! Bangor!" came the singsong chant of the conductor as the engines hissed and the brakes squealed.

It had stopped raining. The platform of the station hovered in long shadows of the setting sun. Was Nana there? Jill hoped she wouldn't have to hang around in the station of a strange town. Her purse tucked under her arm, Jill wrestled with her luggage. Outside, soot and ashes from the steam engine scattered in the wind. The conductor moved her bags to the station platform. "Thank you," Jill said over the noise.

"Jill! Jill!" There was Nana, waving and calling to her. Her blond hair, held back in a fashionable bun, was mixed with silver and shimmered even in the fading sunlight. She wore a white cotton dress and a mint-colored sweater.

Jill bounded off the train. "Nana!" she shrieked, throwing herself into her grandmother's embrace.

"I'm so glad you're here, safe and sound," Nana said after covering Jill's face with kisses. "We'll have a wonderful time together. Look at how tall you've grown since I last saw you!" She eyed Jill's slacks. "Do your mother and father know you're wearing those pants?"

Jill bit her lip. "Um, I bought them after they left," she answered truthfully. "They're very nice for traveling, Nana."

"I see." Nana glanced over Jill's shoulder. "Oh, there's Wendy Taylor! I met her last year when she visited her aunt, Adrie Dekker. My, she's turned into quite a young lady, too. Wendy!" she called. "Come meet my granddaughter, Jill."

Jill whirled around and found herself staring into the flushed face of Scarlett Jones.

3

Embarrassing Moments

Jill could feel her own face redden with humiliation, remembering the fantastic story she had just told Scarlett—or whatever her name was—about her mother being a spy.

Then the embarrassment was replaced with confusion. Wait a minute. Jill wasn't the only one telling lies. Was Scarlett's father really in the film business? Was she an actress? Or were those all lies too?

Nana took hold of the blond girl's hand, pulling her closer. "Wendy," she said, "don't you remember me? Elizabeth Winters? I live out on the harbor road in Winter Haven, not far from your aunt's inn." She motioned to Jill. "This is my granddaughter."

"Wendy?" Jill asked, totally bewildered. "I thought your name was Scarlett."

Scarlett smiled weakly. "Er . . . my friends call me Scarlett. But my real name is Wendy."

Jill felt a surge of anger. "And I suppose your father is not in the film business."

"Yes, he is *so* in the film business!" Wendy retorted.

"Wendy's father runs a movie theater out in New York State," Nana volunteered.

"He runs a movie theater?" Jill's voice rose. "He's not a producer?"

"Well, what about your mother?" Wendy snapped. "Where is she? Off doing some top-secret spy stuff?"

Jill bit her lip, hoping Nana wasn't paying close attention.

Nana looked from one girl to the other. "Did you girls meet on the train?"

"Oh, yes, we met," said Jill, rolling her eyes.

"Well, Jill, I think it's wonderful that you have

a new friend in Winter Haven," said Nana. "Perhaps you'll get together for the big Fourth of July clambake next Saturday. That should be fun." Nana waited for a response, but when neither girl spoke, she asked, "Wendy, do you need a ride?"

"Thank you, but Aunt Adrie should be here any minute to pick me up."

"Then we'll be off." Nana picked up Jill's large bag. "Come on, honey. I know you're tired. You girls can get together later."

Jill grabbed the smaller satchel and started after her grandmother. She glanced back over her shoulder. Wendy was standing there looking miserable—not a bit like the poised, sophisticated girl on the train.

Jill stopped. Maybe . . . maybe Nana was right. Maybe she and Wendy *could* get together for the clambake. After all, there was probably no one to have any fun with in Winter Haven. And what Wendy did certainly wasn't any worse than what Jill had done herself, right?

"Wendy," she called hesitantly, "maybe we *can* do something together sometime. I mean— well—I think we're a lot alike. We were playing the very same game." She smiled weakly. "Only you're better at it than I am."

Wendy sighed. "I feel utterly stupid."

"Coming?" Nana called from the open door.

"Bye," said Jill, turning to leave.

"Jill!" Wendy called after her. "Please come see me at the Tearoom Inn. I really *do* have a job there."

"Okay, I will." Jill paused, then said, "Wendy, my dad really *is* Drew Winters."

"Dreamy!" Wendy responded in awe.

4

The Widow's Walk

Jill awoke the next morning with sunlight and the salty scent of the sea drifting through the open window at the side of her bed. She had fallen asleep in the car on the way to Winter Haven and barely remembered climbing the stairs, undressing, and flopping onto the down quilt.

She rolled over and was startled to see a huge brown-and-black-striped cat curled up at her feet. It stretched out its front legs, yawned, and gazed at Jill through half-closed yellow eyes. "My goodness! Who are you?" Jill asked. "You look more like a raccoon than a cat!" The cat yawned and purred, then rubbed its long silky body against Jill's out-stretched hand.

Taking a deep breath of sea air, Jill got up on her knees and looked through the window. Beyond the rocky coast the Atlantic Ocean sparkled in the sunlight and its colors shifted from deep sapphire blue to smoky shades of green and gray.

Jill unpacked her suitcases. The clothes she brought looked lost in the large closet and bureau. Maybe she and Nana would go shopping in nearby Bayswater someday soon.

She pulled on her slacks, which she had tossed on the chair the night before. After dressing, she headed down the stairs to the kitchen. The cat jumped off the bed and ran ahead of her, holding its bushy tail straight up.

"I see you've met Sarge. He's a real Maine coon cat," Nana explained. "Folks used to think these cats were half raccoon."

"He sure looks like it." Jill bent to stroke the cat, who rubbed against her legs. "He slept with me."

"He's a love, but he's a tough guy," Nana told her. "That's why I named him Sarge. Other cats don't dare to tangle with him, let me tell. And don't be surprised at what he may drag in from outside. He's quite the hunter." Nana set out a folded newspaper on the floor by the sink and put some chicken scraps onto it. Sarge burrowed his face into the meat, pausing now and then to lick his whiskers.

"Nana, Mom said she'd send a telegram when she got to Newfoundland."

"It may be difficult for her. Where she's going there aren't any telephones or electricity."

"When do you get the mail?"

"In the mornings. But it's still early yet."

Jill nodded. "I suppose she hasn't had time to write, anyway."

"Regular mail will be very slow, Jill. Everything coming into the country must be opened and read by censors. Besides, if anything had happened to the *Caribou*, we'd have heard by now. I'm sure she made it across the Gulf safely. Try not to worry."

Jill wasn't only concerned about the Gulf and the U-boats, she wanted to know that Mom wasn't upset with her—that she forgave her for acting so mean. And Jill also wanted Mom to know that she had forgiven *her* for leaving without her.

"Your dad called late last night to be sure you got here safely," Nana said cheerfully. "There's a three-hour difference between here and California. Since the war started, servicemen and military bases have priority to use phones for long distance calls, so civilians must wait their turn. By the time he finally got through, I didn't want to wake you. He sent his love and said he'd try to call sometime next week." Nana put her hand on Jill's shoulder. "But now, you have a surprise."

"I do?"

"Look what I found on the porch this morning." Nana pointed to a small table by the window. In the center was a terra-cotta vase containing a bouquet of bright summer flowers.

"Oh my goodness," Jill said. "Just look at all the roses, snapdragons, and daisies—and those little white things."

"Baby's breath." Nana laughed. "There's a card attached. I didn't open it, but I did see that it's addressed to Miss Jill Winters."

The message on the card was written in green ink. Jill read it out loud. "'Welcome to Winter Haven, Jill. Have a happy vacation.'" Jill looked at her grandmother. "Who do you suppose they're from?"

"I can't imagine."

"They're beautiful." Jill sniffed the flowers.

Nana placed a box of Cheerioats on the large oak table. "I thought you'd like to try this new cereal, if you haven't had them yet." She handed Jill a plate of toast with honey. "Since real butter is rationed, I only use it for Sunday dinners." She wrinkled her nose. "I don't like that oleomargarine stuff. Even with the orange food coloring they give you to whip into it, it reminds me of lard."

Jill was still wondering who sent the flowers as she opened the box of Cheerioats and emptied it along with some milk into a bowl. "What time does the Tearoom Inn open?"

"The tearoom opens at two," said Nana. "Wendy's aunt Adrie will probably have vacationers staying there soon. Although, with the war, I'm not so sure she'll get too many guests."

"Who would be coming way up here to vacation?"

"Folks are saving up their gas stamps for vacations. Others are taking trains, as you did. The town tries to keep things as normal as possible. They were thinking of canceling the annual Fourth of July clambake for the duration but decided to have it after all."

"That's next Saturday! I can hardly wait. I've never been to a real clambake." Jill spooned cereal into her mouth, then stopped. Nana was reaching across the table for her hand.

"We need to remember we're at war, even though we are in a beautiful, peaceful place. If we put your parents in the Lord's hands each morning, you won't need to worry so much."

Embarrassed, Jill swallowed her mouthful of cereal, then bowed her head.

"Lord, please watch over our loved ones in this time of war. Please bring our dear Kate home safely to us. Keep my son, Drew, in the palm of your hand as he shares his gift of song around our country. We pray for peace in our world and love for one another. Amen." Nana squeezed Jill's hand, then let go.

Jill didn't speak during breakfast. Nana's prayer brought a sense of solemnity and even Sarge, who sat on another chair, seemed subdued, his golden eyes half-closed. Nana had put Mom and Dad in the Lord's hands and maybe Jill *could* let go of her worries for today, like Nana said.

After breakfast, Nana took Jill through the house. "I love this place," she said proudly. "But you haven't seen the best part. Come with me." Jill followed her grandmother upstairs and down a hallway. Sarge trotted along behind them. "Wait until you see this!" Nana opened a door, revealing a steep stairway. "Come on!" Nana climbed to the top, then unlatched and shoved open a heavy trapdoor. Cool sea air swept through the passage-way and Sarge darted ahead to the opening above them.

Nana climbed out and Jill scrambled after her onto an open porch that was encircled with a balustrade. "What a beautiful view!" Jill exclaimed.

The ocean glimmered to the east. To the south was a channel from the sea to the safe harbor of Winter Haven. On the other side of the channel a rocky point jutted out even farther into the ocean and on its easternmost cliff stood a majestic white lighthouse. To the west, Jill could see a winding road, a church steeple, and the houses in town.

Ocean swells flung white foam against the northern rocky cliffs that were fringed with pine trees. Pine trees were everywhere and at times their fragrance overpowered the scent of the sea. No wonder Maine was called the Pine Tree State.

"In olden days, the wives of ships' captains would come up to these roofs and watch for their husbands' return from sea." Nana spoke loudly over the sound of the wind. "Many times wives waited and watched and the ship never returned. That's why it's called a *widow's walk*. And then, of course, the wives would watch from these balconies for the kelpies."

"What are kelpies?"

"You don't know? A Scottish legend tells that a kelpie is a black horse with blazing red eyes. It would arise from the ocean and warn sailors' wives of disasters at sea."

"That's scary," Jill said.

"But just imagine their joy when the boats came home safely," Nana said. "I can envision the captains and sailors watching through telescopes for the sight of their wives or sweethearts waving scarves from these rooftops."

"Did anyone ever really see a kelpie?"

"Not anyone I know."

"There's a boat over there!" Jill pointed to a small fishing vessel that rose and dipped in the high waves. She turned to her grandmother. "Can I come up here whenever I want?"

"Of course you can," Nana said. "But this wind is chilly. Let's go down now."

Holding Sarge in her arms, Jill carefully descended the steep stairway, while Nana bolted the trapdoor tightly. "We have to keep it sealed, or it will rain in," she explained.

Back in the kitchen, Nana made a pot of tea then served it on the closed-in sunporch. Windows with flowered chintz curtains and matching window seats stretched along three walls. "I could sit here and look out at the ocean all day long," Nana said. "But at night we need to close all the draperies on our windows that face the sea." She reached up under the valences and pulled a cord. A thick black curtain unfolded and descended from under the valance the full length of one of the windows. "It's the law. Any houses on the ocean must either keep their lights out or cover the windows completely."

"Why? Can they see our lights in Germany?" Jill asked, trying to be silly.

"No, but German submarines could be patrolling these waters, Jill. We don't want to give them any help in identifying landmarks."

"What about the lighthouse? I thought they'd turned the lighthouses off for the duration of the war."

"Some have been turned off, but not all. Ours is one of the few lighthouses that's still working," Nana explained. "They're markers not just for ships, but for airplanes, too. We're so far from big cities or anything important that it's been allowed to stay on, although it's dimmer now."

After tea, Jill helped clean the kitchen, then said, "I'm going to take a walk into town to see Wendy."

"There's a bicycle in the garage, if you'd like to use it."

"A bike! Thanks, Nana." Jill dropped the dish towel on the counter and headed for the side door, which opened to the backyard.

"I hope the tires are okay," Nana said. "I had

them patched and pumped up when I heard you were coming. We can't get new tires because of the rubber shortage." Nana stood in the doorway with Sarge rubbing against her legs as Jill walked toward the garage. "Sometimes you can see the whales breaching from here," she said, pointing to the east.

Jill shaded her eyes and gazed at the ocean.

"Usually you'll see them later in the season," Nana said, "but keep on the watch for them. It's a beautiful sight." She went outside to a water pump and filled a watering can. "Sarge and I plan to do some work in our victory garden this morning." Families everywhere were planting victory gardens to help supplement food that was going to the troops. "See? I've planted peas and tomatoes over there." She pointed, spattering Sarge with the watering can. He shook himself and raced off.

Jill laughed and dashed for the garage. It was a great day for a bike ride! She found the bicycle—a girl's blue Columbia—pulled it out, and checked the tires. She rolled up the legs of her pants a bit, so they wouldn't get caught in the chain.

"Just follow this road to the four corners at Main Street and turn left," Nana called.

Jill hopped on the bicycle. "See you later!" She waved and headed down the dirt road.

She pedaled to town under a cloudless sky. The freshening southerly breeze played with the frothy waves in the harbor. Gulls soared and called to each other. The war seemed far, far away.

5

The Bird Man

Jill found her way into town easily. Except for a path through heavily wooded trees off to the right, there was only one road. At the end of the harbor road, Jill came to a fork. A faded sign showed the words *Main Street*, with a finger pointing to the left. An official-looking government sign indicated that a U.S. Naval Base was a few miles up the road to the right.

Jill took the road to the left and after about a mile found herself on the main street of Winter Haven. Houses and stores lined one side, while across the street were the town docks and the harbor. Wooden fishing boats creaked against the waves and the stiffening breeze; others dotted the water as fishermen were already returning with their morning catch. The scent of salt water and fish drifted in the wind.

She passed the gray fieldstone library. Three girls about Jill's age were coming down the stairs, giggling to one another. As she rode by, Jill smiled tentatively at them. They stopped and stared. Jill could see one of them put her hand to her mouth to whisper something to the others.

Jill kept pedaling down the sidewalk. Outside Guy Binette's grocery store, a man in a white butcher's apron was checking a sign in the window. He backed up, not noticing Jill, and she stopped quickly, her bicycle tottering.

"Whoa! Careful, there!" the man exclaimed, reaching out to help her.

"I'm sorry," Jill apologized. "I probably should be riding in the street."

"Naw, it's safer for you on the sidewalk. But be careful for old-timers like me."

Jill noticed a square flag hanging in the shop window. It was bordered in red with a gold fringe along the bottom. In the center was one blue star on a white field. "I've seen a lot of those flags lately," she said, pointing.

"That there star's fer my son," the grocer said. "My boy Paulie's a soldier. I ain't even sure where he is right now."

"I hope he comes home soon," Jill said. It was hard to know what to say when someone talked about their son in the war.

"So do I. He's all I got left since the missus passed away last winter." The grocer was about to enter the store, but turned to smile at Jill. "I'm the Guy on the sign up there," he said, pointing up. Jill looked confused and the grocer burst out laughing. "I'm the *guy* on the sign—Guy Binette. I own this establishment. *Guy.* Get it?"

Jill laughed. "I get it."

"Now you be careful on that bicycle, young lady."

"I will, Mr. Binette."

He waved and went into the store.

She rode farther up the sidewalk. Another window of Guy's store displayed a poster that read:

SAVE YOUR WASTE FATS
TO MAKE EXPLOSIVES!
GUY GIVES TWO RED
POINTS PER POUND!

Jill's mom collected every drop of fat into a tin can to take to the butcher back home. He awarded two red ration points for every pound of fat too. "With those two red points I can buy an extra pound of sugar," Mom had said, weighing the can on a small scale.

Red and blue stamps in ration books were worth ten points each. A pound of hamburger cost forty-three cents and seven points. A pound of butter, when available, took sixteen points compared to oleomargarine, which took only four. Each ration book contained twenty-eight stamps, which Mom guarded carefully. She worried about burglars breaking into their home for their ration book instead of jewelry or money. They'd illegally sell the books and stamps on the black market, where people were willing to pay lots of money for them.

Jill stopped at the Tearoom Inn and set the

bicycle into a rack by the sidewalk. The large Victorian-style house with its weather-beaten shingles and lacy gingerbread trim stood opposite the harbor wharves. Tiger lilies clustered around a fieldstone wall that bordered the property. Perched on the top gable of the inn, a whale weather vane pointed to the south.

Nana said the tearoom didn't open until two o'clock, but Jill walked briskly up the flagstone path to the wide porch and pushed the brass doorbell, which clanged noisily. No one answered. Jill looked at her watch. Ten-thirty. Surely someone must be up by now.

"They've gone out!" came a call from the street. A boy in a white sailor's cap and a plaid shirt stood by a parked car with a bucket of paint and a paintbrush. "You just missed 'em."

Jill headed back to the sidewalk.

"You're new in town, ain't ya?" asked the boy. He set the paint down and took off his cap. Strands of red hair blew across his forehead and into his green eyes. He seemed to be about sixteen or so. "I'll bet you're Mrs. Winters's granddaughter."

Jill nodded. "Yes, I'm Jill Winters. How'd you know?"

"Your grandma said you'd be comin'. I'm Quarry MacDonald. Live out to Lighthouse Road. My pa's the lighthouse keeper."

Quarry is an odd name, Jill thought.

As if reading her mind, Quarry said, "Quarry's a Scottish name. It means 'proud.' MacDonald's Scottish too. My grandparents were from Nova Scotia, which, in case you don't know, means 'New Scotland.'" He gestured to his paint can. "I'm goin' around paintin' the top half o' car headlights black—in case of an air raid. Most everyone's got 'em done by now, but some are chippin' and need a touch-up. Folks pay me a half a buck to do their lights."

"I wouldn't worry about air raids in these parts," Jill said. "Who'd bomb Winter Haven? It's not a big city with airplane factories or anything. It's just a little fishing village."

"No, it ain't a big city, that's a fact, but we're obeyin' the law by paintin' the top half of head-lights, just the same. Are you lookin' for Wendy?"

"Yes, I am."

"Well, as I said, she just went out with her aunt in their fancy car." He slammed his hat over his head, capturing wayward wisps of hair under it.

Jill pulled her bicycle from the stand. "I'll be heading back, then."

"I heard from the grapevine your mother's crossin' the Gulf to Newfoundland. Pretty scary with all those U-boats, you know. Did ya hear today's news? They sunk another merchant ship down the coast."

"Thanks for telling me," Jill snapped.

The boy shifted from one long, lanky leg to the other. "Sorry," he muttered, looking down. "I shouldn't-a said that. You're probably right worried about your ma."

"Of course I am, but I'm sure she's safe in Newfoundland by now. I would have heard if something happened." Jill tried to sound convincing.

"That's right. Say, I hear your pa's that big Herb, Drew Winters. Good Godfrey! How's it feel to have a famous pa?" When Jill didn't answer, Quarry went on. "He travels a lot. I s'pose you worry 'bout him, too. Bein' on planes so much and all those saboteurs tryin' to blow things up . . ."

"I'm trying *not* to worry, thank you," Jill said as she pulled herself onto the bicycle seat.

"Oops, leave it to me to put my foot in my mouth," Quarry said meekly. "Sorry."

He picked up the paint can and started up the street to the next parked car.

U-boats! Saboteurs! Jill headed toward her grandmother's house. When she passed Quarry, she pretended she didn't see him wave to her.

Jill was more than halfway home and rounding a bend in the road when her front wheel hit a rock. POP! The tire blew! The handlebars jerked in her grasp and the bicycle veered uncontrollably. She screamed as the bike slipped and skidded, tipping her onto the loose gravel.

"Oh, darn!" Jill wailed as she pulled herself from under the bicycle. Her knees were smarting and she felt a trickle of blood down her left leg. Jill was dismayed to see a rip and a brownish-red stain oozing through the knee of her slacks.

She got up, pulled the bicycle to the side of the road, and rolled the leg of her pants above her bleeding knee. She looked around and realized she was near the driveway of an old bungalow. A dusty tan station wagon was parked in a run-down garage next to the house. Maybe someone here could help her. If she could use the telephone, Nana would come and pick her up.

Jill leaned the bicycle against the post-and-rail fence and went to the side door. There was no bell, so she knocked hesitantly. When no one answered she knocked harder.

The gash on her knee stung and blood had started soaking into her sock and sneaker. Maybe there was water or a hose around somewhere.

She hobbled toward the back of the house and found a hand pump on a cement pedestal. Jill removed her shoe and sock, then pumped the handle vigorously until water gushed. She held her bruised knee under the flow and gritted her teeth until the icy water numbed the pain.

When she was finished she sat on the cement, stretching her bare leg to dry in the sunshine. In the backyard, beyond the lawn, she could see what looked like a chicken coop. The whooshing sound of wind in the nearby pines mixed with the cooing of the birds. Why, they're not chickens, Jill realized. They're pigeons! Her leg was dry now and her knee had stopped bleeding. She put on her sock and sneaker and wandered over to the coop.

Twenty or more birds of various shades cooed and fluttered around the cage, which was covered with a mesh wire. Some pecked and trotted on the ground while others poked their heads through little round holes of a dovecote that was part of the enclosure.

Jill walked around to the other side of the cage. The back of the pigeon coop abutted the wire mesh, but on this side there were shelves with sliding doors. Why would anyone want to keep pigeons? She thought about the parks in Boston and the dirty birds that followed visitors, looking for handouts of peanuts, or messing all over the statues. Jill tapped her fingers against the mesh wire. A few birds fluttered and scattered.

"Hey! Leave them birds alone!" A dark-haired man suddenly appeared from the house. His long legs brought him quickly to the pigeon coop, and his face was flushed as he charged toward Jill. "What are you doing?" He confronted her, his hands on his hips. "Can't you read signs?"

"I didn't see any sign," she stammered. "I fell

off my bike and I needed some help." She pointed to her knee. "I . . . I knocked on the door, but no one answered so I washed my leg off at your pump, that's all."

"I didn't hear anyone knock." He glared at her accusingly. "What were you doing to the birds?"

"I was only looking at them." Jill backed away and the man followed her. "I'm leaving now," she said, heading for the driveway.

"There's the sign!" The man pointed to a board that stood between the garage and the walkway to the backyard. NO TRESPASSING was crudely lettered in black paint.

"I didn't see it. I was too busy being hurt!" Jill's voice rose. "I thought somebody might help me, but I guess I was wrong!"

The man backed down a little. "Do you want to use the phone?"

"No." There was no way that Jill would enter the house with this man. "I'll walk back to my grandmother's." She indicated the direction up the road with her hand. "Sorry to bother you," she said.

"Your grandmother? Would that be Elizabeth Winters?"

"Yes. I'm Jill Winters. I'm living with my grandmother while my parents are away." Jill marched down the driveway and pulled her bicycle from the fence.

"I'm Clayton Bishop. Sorry if I was abrupt," the man called as he trailed her. "I was worried about my birds."

"I don't think anyone's interested in your pigeons."

"They're valuable birds," Clayton explained. "I breed them . . . for food."

"Pigeons? For food?"

"They're better known in restaurants as *squab*. A real delicacy." The man stood at the end of his driveway. "I can call your grandmother if you'd like."

"No thank you. I'll be all right." She headed up the road toward her grandmother's house, pushing the bicycle slowly and awkwardly on the gravel. Just before the road curved, she turned to look back.

Clayton Bishop was still standing in the driveway watching her.

6

Adrie

The sun was bearing down hard when Jill finally arrived home. Her left knee was smarting as dust from the road mixed with salty sweat and blood. In the driveway, Nana's station wagon with its faded wood paneling looked shabby next to a new tan Chrysler coupe.

Who's here? Jill wondered as she maneuvered her bicycle past the cars, into the garage.

Nana opened the kitchen door and called to her. "Come in, Jill. Wendy and her aunt are here to see you." She left the door open and went back into the house.

Jill rolled her slacks down over her dusty legs. Her shirt was wringing wet with perspiration and her hair clung to her face and neck in limp ringlets. She went into the kitchen where the tall ceiling captured the hot air and left the living area cool and dry. Voices were coming from the sunporch. Hastily she washed her face with the cold water from the stone sink, then went out to the porch.

Wendy and her aunt were sitting on a sofa. Sarge was on the window seat, washing his face.

"Where were you?" Nana asked, looking her over. "What happened?"

"I had an accident with the bike." Jill pulled up the leg of her slacks and pointed to her scraped knee. "The tire blew out on a rock . . ."

"Oh my goodness, that's too bad!" Nana exclaimed, getting up to look more closely at Jill's knee. "I was afraid those tires wouldn't hold up. What a shame! Your first morning here and you get hurt." She went into the kitchen.

"We must have passed you on the road," Wendy said. "Jill, I'd like you to meet my aunt, Adrie Dekker."

"How do you do, Miss Dekker?" Jill said to the pretty smiling woman. Jill noticed that, except for the color of their eyes—Wendy's being turquoise and Adrie's dark brown—there was a strong resemblance between the two, right down to that single dimple that appeared when they smiled.

"Hello, Jill. We thought we'd come over to see you before the tearoom opened," Miss Dekker explained, glancing at her watch. She wore a rose-colored print dress with a white Peter Pan collar, which didn't look a bit childish. In fact, Jill imagined that this woman, like Wendy, could make any clothes look glamorous. Miss Dekker spoke in a quiet voice with hardly a trace of a Maine accent. "We don't have a lot of customers this early in the season. It's when we have guests and serve three meals a day that it becomes hectic." Miss Dekker looked Jill up and down, then held out her hand. "It's a pleasure to meet you, Jill. And please call me Adrie. Most folks here in town use first names."

"Thank you . . . Adrie. It's nice to meet you, too." Jill shook Adrie's hand and noticed she was wearing a gold ring with a large red stone. "What a beautiful ring."

"It is beautiful," Adrie agreed. "It's a rare pigeon blood ruby—my July birthstone. It will be Wendy's someday—when I'm gone."

"Don't say that!" Wendy exclaimed. "Don't ever talk about dying. I couldn't stand it if anything happened to you!"

Jill was startled at Wendy's reaction.

Her aunt also seemed surprised. "I just meant that you're my only niece—my sister's daughter—and your birthday's in July too."

Wendy looked at the floor. "I . . . I'm sorry. That's nice of you, Aunt Adrie, to think of me."

"I wouldn't dream of leaving this ring to anyone else." Adrie turned to Jill. "Jill, you have a strong resemblance to your famous father."

"We think Jill looks very much like her beautiful mother," Nana called from the kitchen. "They both have those wonderful honey-colored eyes."

Jill flushed. Yes! Mom *was* beautiful. She had a quiet, royal bearing, yet she was fun, too. She and Dad loved going on surprise trips, treasure hunts, and stargazing picnics. Jill ached as she thought about her mother. How she wished she were here!

Adrie interrupted Jill's thoughts. "Jill *is* quite pretty."

Jill certainly didn't feel pretty, especially when Wendy was around. Today Wendy wore a bright red-and-white-striped shirt with a sailor collar and matching red tie. Her navy blue shorts matched her canvas shoes.

Nana came back carrying a box of bandages and a bottle of iodine. "Too bad there was no one to help you when you fell."

"I stopped for help at that little cottage down the road—the one with the birds."

"Birds?" Nana asked as she knelt in front of Jill. "I don't know anyone with birds." She painted Jill's cut with iodine, then placed a bandage over it.

"I knocked at the door, but no one answered, so I went out back to wash off my knee. A man came out of the house and yelled at me. He told me to leave the birds alone. He seemed to know who you were, Nana," said Jill, wincing as her wound began to sting.

"Oh, yes. I think his name is Bishop. He's new around these parts," said Nana. "I hardly know him."

"Clayton Bishop," Jill told her. "Don't have anything to do with him, Nana. He's pretty mean."

Wendy's aunt straightened her dress around her knees. "Wendy, don't you want to make some plans with Jill? That's why you came out here." Jill thought she sounded annoyed. "Otherwise, let's head back now."

"Can't you leave me here?" asked Wendy. "I can walk back later. It's still early and I'll get back long before two."

Jill glanced over at her grandmother, who raised her eyebrows in a silent question. Jill nodded and Nana said, "Do stay and visit, Wendy. We'll have lunch and then I'll drive you to the inn by one o'clock. Will that be all right?" she asked Adrie.

Adrie got up to leave. "That will be fine. And Wendy, don't be a pest."

Nana and the girls walked out to the driveway while Adrie got into her car.

"This car is a beauty! It's so streamlined—like a bullet!" Nana said admiringly, as she peeked into the front seat. "You were fortunate to get this before the government's ban on making new cars."

"Luck *was* with me," Adrie said through the open window.

"Were you on a waiting list?" Nana asked.

"Hm? Oh, yes." Adrie seemed preoccupied as she started the engine.

"Does this have that newfangled transmission I've been hearing about?" Nana called out. "Fluid drive?"

Adrie nodded and, looking over her shoulder, backed up the car.

"Maybe I can drive it sometime," Wendy said eagerly.

Adrie waved as she drove off down the road, the dust billowing up behind her.

"I'm going to make us a nice lunch," Nana said.

"Can we help?" Jill asked.

"Why don't you two go sit out on the rocks while I put things together. You can eat outside. I'll ring the bell when it's ready." Nana headed into the house.

"Come on." Jill, ignoring her throbbing knee, pulled Wendy by the hand. They crossed the lawn and climbed onto the rocks that jutted out toward the ocean, then stopped before reaching the place where the high tide came in and the rocks became green and slippery.

"This is far enough." Jill settled down on a large flat boulder and put her sore leg out straight. "Oh, look!" She reached into a crevasse that was filled with tidewater and pulled out a tiny snail. "Here's a periwinkle," she said, holding it for Wendy to see. "Watch this." Jill began to sing an old Newfoundland verse her mother had taught her. "*Periwinkle, Periwinkle, show your horns. If you don't, I'll kill your mother, father, sister, brother, all you have belonging to you.*"

"That's awful," Wendy complained. "It's cruel."

"Shh. Whenever we go to the beach back home we always do this. Watch." Jill held her mouth closer to the shell in her hand and sang the verse again, softly. The hole where the shellfish was hiding slowly opened as the snail emerged, showing hornlike protrusions.

"Holy moley! Look at that!" Wendy exclaimed. At the sound of her voice the periwinkle pulled itself back into the shell.

"You scared it." Jill replaced the snail into the little tide pool between the rocks.

"I guess I bother everyone," Wendy complained. "Even the snails." She looked out to sea, and Jill wondered if she was about to cry. "I hope Aunt Adrie doesn't think I'm a bother. She's usually nice to me, but sometimes I feel like I'm in the way. Did you hear her call me a pest?"

Jill didn't know how to answer. Then she whispered, "You're not a pest, Wendy."

The waves surged over the rocks beyond them and gulls soared overhead. Jill recalled her grandmother describing how this whole point was covered with water during storms.

After a long silence, Wendy suddenly spoke up. "Someone must like me. We found a beautiful bouquet of flowers on the doorstep this morning. It had a card addressed to me that said, 'Welcome to Winter Haven, Wendy. Have a wonderful vacation.'"

"I got a bouquet too!" Jill noticed a flash of disappointment cross Wendy's face and she almost regretted telling her. "Was there any name on your card?"

"No. I have no idea who sent it."

"Me neither," said Jill.

"I thought it might be from a boy up here who I think likes me."

"I'll bet lots of boys like you."

Wendy nodded. "Yes, they do."

"Where are you from, Wendy? Really."

"I'm from upper New York State. A small town called Derry. You probably never heard of it."

"What do your parents do?"

"Well, as your grandmother told you, my dad runs a movie theater. He's too old to be in the service. He's in his fifties. How come your dad's not in the service? He looks young."

"My dad has a bad ear. Would you believe it? I mean, here he is a singer and he has a bad ear. He had an ear operation once and now he gets dizzy spells."

"Then your dad is a 4-F. He didn't pass the physical and that's why he's not in the army." Wendy looked thoughtful. "Beethoven became totally deaf. Imagine never being able to hear your own music."

Wendy seemed to know a lot. "Tell me about your mother," Jill said.

"Mom's never around. She's too busy with her clubs. She's always doing charity drives and now they're making up Bundles for Britain—you know, for people who've lost everything in the bombings." Wendy rolled her eyes. "It's important, I guess, but sometimes I feel as if she's too busy to have me around. I heard Mom tell Dad, 'Why don't we send Wendy up to Adrie's for the summer? It will be good for both of them.' They never even asked me if I wanted to come. It was a fait accompli."

Jill wondered what a *fait accompli* was but decided not to ask. "I kind of feel the same way," Jill confessed. "My mother went off to Newfoundland and she wouldn't take me. She's risking her life for her brother—my uncle Cliff—and I honestly wonder if she cares more about him than she does about *me*."

"What about your dad? Couldn't you be with him? It'd be swell traveling around with your father in show business and everything."

"No, Dad won't take me on his tours. He said it wouldn't be safe for me to travel around the country." Jill picked up a shell and tossed it into the tide pool. "I'll probably have to spend the whole summer here—or at least until my mom comes home."

"Well, we can have fun together."

"Maybe we can go shopping in Bayswater," Jill suggested. "But you've already got lots of nice clothes."

Wendy looked down at her smart outfit and seemed to brighten. "Isn't this cute? Mom said it was 'nautical. The perfect thing for the seashore.'" Wendy's voice went into a snooty imitation of whom Jill assumed was her mother.

"So tell me about your aunt. What is she like?"

"Isn't she beautiful? I wish I could look just like her."

"You do look like her," Jill said. "Except her eyes are brown."

"Oh, thank you, Jill. She's *beautiful*," Wendy said again. "Wasn't that nice of her—telling me I would have her gorgeous ring someday? But I hope that day never comes. I don't know what I'd do if anything happened to Adrie. I suppose it's an awful thing to say, but sometimes I wish she were my mother—even if she sometimes thinks I'm a pest."

There was an awkward silence, then Jill said, "Adrie's nice."

"She doesn't talk about herself much," Wendy said. "She's mysterious—like that movie star Greta Garbo."

Jill nodded. "Well I know someone who talks a *lot*! I met Quarry MacDonald when I went down to find you at the inn. He said you had gone out with your aunt."

"He must have been watching for me. I thought he might have been the person who sent me the flowers." A quick smile crossed Wendy's face.

"Well, I'm sure he didn't send them to me. Still, he knew all about my mother going across the Gulf. He told me about the U-Boats, and then he went on to warn me about saboteurs blowing up planes! As if I wasn't already worried. My dad takes planes all the time. What a dumb thing to say."

Wendy shrugged. "Well, Quarry's outspoken. That's the way people are around here. But he's quite nice-looking, don't you think?"

"I didn't notice," Jill answered. "He just made me so mad."

Clang! Clang! Jill jumped up. "Nana's bell! Come on. I don't know about you, but I'm starved."

The girls sat at a picnic table out on the lawn where Nana served up a platter of egg salad sandwiches, a bowl of potato chips, and a pitcher of frosty chocolate milk.

"I had the salad all made when I realized I was out of bread," Nana said, as she handed each girl a plate. "So I drove up to the grocery store."

Jill helped herself to the chips. "That was fast."

"Wendy, does your aunt know that new man—Clayton Bishop?" Nana looked puzzled.

"I don't know. Why?" Wendy asked.

"When we were talking about him this morning, she never mentioned that she knew him." Nana sat down on the picnic bench. "I was a little curious about Clayton Bishop, after hearing how nasty he was to Jill. So as I drove to the store I looked more closely at his cottage. I could swear I caught a glimpse of Adrie's Chrysler parked out in the back of the house."

7

Shadows

"I don't think Aunt Adrie knows him," Wendy said. "At least, she's never mentioned him to me."

"Maybe she was ordering squab for the inn," Jill suggested. "She said she'd be starting meals soon. Clayton Bishop said he raises pigeons for food."

"Perhaps so. You don't need to use ration stamps for pigeons," Nana said. "But if you're hungry, you'd probably need to eat four squab. There's hardly any meat on them."

Jill shuddered. "I've never eaten a pigeon and

I don't think I ever will—even when they're called *squab*."

"Oh, but I've heard they serve them at all the ritzy restaurants," Wendy said.

Nana reached for a potato chip. "Jill, tonight's my night out. Every Sunday night I meet with friends. I'm hoping you'll be able to keep yourself busy on Sunday evenings without me."

"It's okay, Nana. I listen to my favorite radio programs every Sunday. I'll be fine."

Nana nodded. "Good."

"I love Charlie McCarthy!" said Wendy. "He's on Sunday nights."

"What do you do with your friends?" Jill asked her grandmother. "Play cards?"

"No, we just talk," Nana said. She got up and took the empty plates from the table and headed inside.

"Can you come over on Sunday nights?" Jill asked Wendy.

"Right after I help with the dinner dishes." Wendy heaved a sigh. "There's only Aunt Adrie and me right now. I hope we don't have too many guests at the inn this summer. I don't want to miss the clambake and the dances coming up." Wendy looked over Jill's shoulder. "Say, look who's come to visit."

Quarry MacDonald was standing in the driveway by his bicycle. "What's he doing here?" Jill whispered.

"He's probably following me," Wendy answered under her breath. "I told you he likes me."

Quarry waved and adjusted the kickstand on the bicycle. "Hi!" he said, coming into the yard. "Just thought I'd drop by to say hello." He sat down on the picnic bench. "Guess I missed lunch—and me hungry enough to eat a boiled owl."

"Too bad," Jill said.

Quarry ignored her comment. "Hey, what are you two doin' tonight?"

"Why?" Wendy asked.

Quarry spoke directly to Jill. "I know your grandma meets with the other witchy ladies on Sunday nights, so I figured you'd be alone and wonderin' what to do."

Jill frowned. "What do you mean, 'witchy ladies'?"

"That's what everyone calls 'em. They have

secret meetings at Ida Wilmar's house. No one knows what's goin' on. It's been kinda suspicious for round about a year now."

"What do you mean *suspicious*?" Jill demanded. "Can't some ladies get together and knit or something without the whole town wondering what's going on?"

Quarry shrugged. "Word gets round this town. Lots of blabber mouths in Winter Haven."

"The ladies are probably knitting afghans. All the club women back home are making afghans for servicemen," Wendy said. "There must be enough afghans for everyone in the world by now."

"Don't forget Bundles for Britain," Jill added. "My mom keeps a big barrel in the garage and we fill it every month with clothes and blankets to send overseas."

"Oh well, it's no one's business what those ladies do, anyway," Wendy said. She turned to Quarry. "What are *you* doing tonight? Jill and I thought we'd listen to Charlie McCarthy. Want to come over?"

"Is it okay, Jill?" Quarry asked.

"I guess so," Jill said reluctantly. "I'll have to ask Nana first."

"Ask me what?" Nana appeared from the house with more dishes and a pie. "Dessert is ready. Hello, Quarry. Want a slice of apple pie?"

"Quarry wants to listen to the radio with us tonight while you're gone," Jill explained. "Is that all right, Nana?"

"It's fine by me." Nana slid pieces of pie onto the plates. She handed Jill a wedge of Gouda cheese and a knife. "Cut this up four ways," she said. "It tastes good enough to eat, with apple pie."

"I'll do it," Wendy offered, slicing the cheese and placing a piece on each plate.

Shortly after Nana left for the evening, Quarry and Wendy arrived. Jill turned on the radio in the parlor and they listened to the Jack Benny and Charlie McCarthy programs. They sipped soda pop and ate molasses cookies that Nana made with the last of her month's supply of sugar. Sarge took a fancy to Quarry and stretched out at his feet like a dog.

"Will your dad be singing on the radio sometime soon, Jill?" asked Wendy.

"He said he'd be on *Manhattan Merry-Go-Round* soon. That's on Sunday nights too."

"Swell, we'll come over and listen with you," said Wendy.

"It must be great to have a famous dad," Quarry said. "But you ain't stuck-up, Jill."

"What's to be stuck-up about?" Jill replied. "My dad's a pretty regular person. It's hard to think of him as a celebrity."

"What's he like?" Wendy asked. "I mean . . . *really*."

"He's . . . nice. He's fun. I miss him when he's away. But he always sends me little gifts wherever he is. Sometimes when he's on the air, he sings certain songs especially for Mom."

"What songs?" asked Quarry.

"'You're My Everything' and 'Our Love is Here to Stay' and . . ."

Wendy sighed. "That is so utterly romantic."

"When I was born, Daddy sang 'Mighty Like a Rose' on the radio. Actually, that song is written for a boy baby, so Daddy changed it a little, for a girl. All my birth announcements had a rose on them." Jill became quiet.

Quarry got up to look out the window. "It's just now gettin' dark and it's almost nine o'clock. Hey, there's somethin' way out there on the water."

Jill jumped up and ran to the windows. "Probably a whale. Nana says sometimes you can see them breach out front."

"There, see?" Quarry pointed to a shadow off the point. "If it were a whale breachin', it would have disappeared by now."

Jill could only see dark waves. "Don't they come in schools?"

"Pods," Wendy joined them. "Whales are in *pods*."

"What I mean is, if there's one we may see others. Let's go up to the widow's walk and watch." Jill ran to the stairs. "Come on!"

The trio raced up the stairway leading to the lookout. "Be careful," Jill said as she led the way to the rooftop. She tugged at the heavy bolt, then pushed the hatch door open.

"This is some sight!" Quarry exclaimed when they stepped onto the deck. "It's 'bout as good a view as from the top o' the lighthouse. You can even see the entrance to Frenchman's Cove from here."

"Where's that?" Wendy asked.

"Over there on the other side o' those cliffs." Quarry pointed. "It's a nice gunkhole."

"What's a gunkhole?" Jill asked.

"It's a hidden harbor—bigger 'n an eel rut."

"Speak English, Quarry!" Jill exclaimed. "I don't understand you!"

"I'm talkin' English, for Pete's sake!" Quarry spouted.

"It's just Maine talk," Wendy said to Jill. Then, addressing Quarry, she said, "Now explain what an eel rut is."

"An eel rut's a tiny inlet. But Frenchman's Cove is deep—a gunkhole. It's got the deepest water round here. In fact, I heard say it's the only natural fjord in North America."

"What's a fjord?" Jill asked.

"Danged if I know." Quarry laughed. "A hole, I reckon."

"It's a deep gorge under the water," Wendy said. "Norway is known for its fjords."

"You're right smart, Wendy," Quarry said.

"Anyways, Frenchman's Cove's deserted. No way to get in or out of there by foot, 'cept by an old path through the woods."

Jill went to the railing. "There! I see something moving through the waves! Look! In that glow on the water from the lighthouse beam. See?"

Quarry squinted his eyes. "That ain't no whale."

"I don't see it," said Wendy.

Jill scanned the water. "Neither do I, now."

"Was it a boat?" asked Wendy.

"Maybe, but it had no lights," Jill answered.

"Sometimes fishermen come back to the harbor without lights. That way they can't be spotted by enemy subs. You know, U-boats," Quarry explained.

"U-boats. Unterseeboote," Wendy said. "That's German for . . ."

"Undersea boats," said Jill wearily. "That's easy enough to figure out."

"There are no enemy subs around here," Wendy scoffed. "They're out on the ocean looking for warships, not fishermen."

"We got a Naval Intelligence Radio Intercept

Station just down the road a piece. They're listenin' for subs all the time," said Quarry. "If there
was any U-boats out there, they'd be in touch with
each other by radio. The naval base'd hear anything comin' across on radio waves."

"So you're sure there are no U-boats around
here?" Jill asked.

"Positive," said Quarry. "My pa would have
heard somethin' about it from the coast guard. He
hears all the news. That's how I found out about
the ship that was lost t'other night. It'd be dumb
for U-boats to be cruisin' these here parts, with the
navy listenin' right up the road. Wendy's right.
U-boats ain't interested in fishermen."

"Well, whatever it was, it's gone," said Jill.
"Let's go downstairs. I'm getting cold."

"But it's so pretty out here," said Wendy, holding her skirt and twirling around. "I wish I were a
bird. I'd fly right to the moon." As she pranced,
her dress fluttered in the breeze like wings.
"Come on and dance, Quarry!" she teased, tug-
ging him by his sleeve.

Quarry pulled away. "Aw, for Pete's sake,
Wendy. Cut it out."

"Let's go inside," Jill said. "I'm freezing."

"How about makin' some cocoa, Jill?" Quarry suggested.

"Okay." Jill turned once more to the east. Mom must have made it safely across the Gulf. What was it that people who have sons fighting in the war said? *No news is good news.* Jill would have heard if something bad had happened, wouldn't she? But Mom still had to cross the dangerous waters once more, when she came back to the States.

Please don't let the U-boats find Mom's ship, Jill prayed silently.

8

Truth, Dare, Consequences, Promise, or Repeat

Jill made hot chocolate and served it in china teacups. Quarry pretended to be a French waiter with a tea towel folded over one arm. He took Jill's vase of flowers and placed them in the center of the table. Jill was tempted to ask if he had sent them but changed her mind. He bowed deeply and served the cocoa to the girls at the kitchen table. "Here you are, mademoiselles," he said, faking a French accent.

Wendy giggled. "Aunt Adrie should hire you for our tearoom, monsieur." She began talking about her friends in New York. "My best friend back home is Barbara. Her father is a senator. Barbara is a debutante. She had a huge coming-out party and of course I was invited. I wore a gorgeous full-length dress of sheer white georgette."

Jill wondered what georgette was. She also wondered how much of Wendy's story was true. But it didn't really matter. Wendy and Quarry were fun and it seemed that Winter Haven might be a nice place to spend the summer after all.

"Tell me what goes on here in the summer," Jill asked.

"Well, you know 'bout the Fourth of July clambake comin' up this Saturday," Quarry began. "That'll be down on the beach. O'course there won't be fireworks 'cause of the war, but everyone in town'll be there. Then Saturday night dances will be startin' up next week at Grange Hall. They're lotsa fun."

"I went to those dances a couple of times last year, but the girls who live here are snobs." Wendy pushed her nose up with her finger. "They called me 'one of those *summercaters*.'"

Jill recalled the three girls in town who had whispered about *her*. "Summercaters?"

"Summer people. Folks from away who come down east to vacation," Quarry explained. "The local folks don't take kindly to summer people." He looked sheepish. "But I ain't like that."

"No, you don't treat us that way," said Wendy. "You know, many folks around here would be out of business if it weren't for 'summercaters' like us."

"There's another big formal dance that's like a prom," Quarry continued. "The Crystals and Rocks put it on up in Ellsworth every summer. They call it the Crystal Ball. But you gotta be invited to that. The most popular girls round here belong to the Crystals. The boys belong to the Rocks. They're the big Herbs in town. They meet at the church a couple times a month."

"Can anyone join?" Jill asked.

"No. First, someone has to sponsor you. Then you gotta show up at a special meetin' where everyone sizes you up. If you pass inspection, they vote on whether they'll let you join or not. They have a box with white and black balls. Each person votes by puttin' in a white ball or a blackball. If there's even one blackball in the box, you're out. Nobody ever discovers who blackballed 'em."

"Have you been asked to join?" Wendy asked.

Quarry shrugged. "Naw, they'd never invite me."

"Why not? They're only country folk like you . . ." Wendy stopped and looked embarrassed. "I'm sorry, Quarry. There's nothing wrong with being country folk. What I mean is . . . they're not any *better* than you. They're not rich, big-city socialites or anything."

"It makes 'em feel important, I guess," Quarry answered. "I don't want to join, anyhow."

"Neither do I," said Jill.

"What do they do in their club?" Wendy asked.

"Oh, they have war bond drives. The Rocks collect cans and steel and wash cars. The girls make cookies to send to the troops. Some of them knit scarves and mittens for servicemen. They have their pictures in the local papers all the time."

"I'd like to belong to the Crystals. It might be fun, but I suppose we don't have a chance." Wendy sounded disappointed.

"I guess that's just the way people are around here. I can't help but wonder why Nana ever chose to move away from all her friends in

Boston to live in this faraway place," Jill said.

"Yep, until you came she was all stark alone in this big house," Quarry agreed.

"The landscape is beautiful here," said Wendy. "She probably likes the peace and quiet."

"I've wondered why your aunt Adrie lives here," said Quarry. "She's so good-lookin' and smart. Folks say she speaks several languages."

Wendy nodded. "Aunt Adrie speaks French, Spanish, and German. She has traveled all over Europe, but she was born in New York State, like my mother."

"It does seem strange that anyone as sophisticated as your aunt would want to live up here in the country," said Jill.

"She has a good business, especially in the summer," Wendy replied. "She doesn't seem to have many friends, though. I don't know why."

"People in town think she's icebound," Quarry said. "She's kind of a tiptoe Nancy."

Wendy drew herself up angrily. "What's that supposed to mean!"

"She ain't too friendly," Quarry said. "She puts on airs."

"They're just jealous," Wendy snapped.

"Well, you asked why she ain't got friends, so I told you." Quarry turned his attention to Jill. "But your grandmother has her Sunday-night ladies, Jill. And did you know her pal Ida Wilmar is a *German*?" Quarry asked. "Most folks stay clear of Ida. They don't like Germans these days."

"Just because she's German doesn't mean she's a Nazi!" Jill declared.

"I suppose so," said Quarry, looking uncomfortable. "It's just that—well, like I say, people talk round here, Jill." Quarry grinned weakly. "Forget it. Let's play a game."

"What game?" Wendy asked.

"Um, how about Truth, Dare, Consequences, Promise, or Repeat?" Quarry suggested.

"That'll be fun," Jill agreed.

"I hosey to go first," Quarry said.

"Okay. Which will it be?" Wendy asked, "Truth, Dare, Consequences, Promise, or Repeat?"

"I'll start with *repeat*," he answered. "It's least dangerous."

"Repeat after me," Wendy ordered. "I, Quarry

MacDonald, think that Wendy and Jill are the prettiest girls in Winter Haven."

Jill laughed as she watched a flush creep over Quarry's face. "I, Quarry MacDonald, think that Wendy and Jill are the prettiest girls in Winter Haven," he repeated.

"Now it's your turn, Wendy," said Jill. "What'll it be? Truth, Dare, Consequences, Promise, or Repeat?"

Wendy hesitated. "Truth," she said.

Jill thought for a moment, then asked, "Do your friends back home really call you Scarlett?"

Wendy looked embarrassed. "No," she admitted. "I just . . . like to pretend it's my name."

"And what about your aunt Adrie?" Quarry asked. "How do you feel about her? Remember, you've gotta tell the truth."

Wendy frowned. "I thought I would get only one question."

"Okay, fair enough," said Quarry. "Now it's your turn, Jill. Which is it? Truth, Dare, Consequences, Promise, or Repeat?"

"Promise," Jill said.

"Promise this," said Quarry. "I will be a faithful friend to Wendy and Quarry."

Jill put up her right hand, as if taking an oath. "I promise to be a faithful friend to Wendy and Quarry."

"No matter what," Wendy added.

"No matter what," Jill promised.

Quarry leaned back. "This ain't excitin' enough. Let's do a dare. Who'll go first?"

"I will!" Jill said eagerly. "I love a dare."

Wendy waved her hands. "I have the perfect dare for Jill. I dare you to get us into the Crystals!"

"That's not fair," Jill grumbled. "You said we didn't stand a chance. We're summer people. They won't let us in."

"They will—when they learn that your father is the famous Drew Winters!" Wendy insisted. "They'll beg you to join. And you'll get them to invite me, too." She turned to Quarry. "You'll have to introduce us to those snobby girls, Quarry. Then it's up to Jill."

Jill sank back in her chair. "I didn't think you'd give me anything so tough. Besides, I'm not sure I want to join the Crystals."

"You said you loved a dare," Quarry reminded her.

"Okay," Jill said with a resigned sigh. "I'll try."

"I'll introduce you to Betty Whitfield, Elaine O'Brien, and Gloria Brandt. They're the big three that run everything," said Quarry. "Elaine is the 'honorable counselor of the Crystals.'" He rolled his eyes. "And she don't let anyone forget it, neither. They'll be at Youth Fellowship at the church next Sunday afternoon. Betty's the president." Quarry paused. "Do you go to church, Jill? I know your grandmother doesn't."

"There you go again! I can't believe that you keep such close watch on my grandmother!" Jill got up, nearly knocking over her chair. "You want to know what she does on Sunday nights. You repeat gossip about her friends. You wonder why she doesn't go to church. Is there anything else you want to know?"

"Quarry didn't mean to make you mad," Wendy said soothingly.

"That's right. Don't get all in a lather, Jill," Quarry begged. "I'm right sorry."

"You should be!" Jill declared angrily. Car

lights glimmered in the kitchen window. "Nana's home. Why don't you ask her yourself?"

The kitchen door opened and Nana bustled in. "What a beautiful moon out there!" She stopped and looked from Jill to Wendy to Quarry. "Is everything all right?"

"Yes," Jill answered. She smiled, but sent daggers in her glare at Quarry. "Quarry is just going home."

"Do you want a ride?" Nana asked.

"No, thanks, Mrs. Winters. I have my bike."

"Well, be careful out there in the dark," Nana cautioned.

"I will." Quarry stood by the door, shifting from one foot to the other. "Good night."

Wendy and Nana each said "Good night" but Jill was silent. Quarry shot one final, pleading glance at her, then went out the door.

9

Sonnabend IV

After Quarry left, Jill asked, "Nana, can Wendy stay over?"

"Certainly," Nana responded. "But do get permission from her aunt first."

"Aunt Adrie said it's fine with her," Wendy said, after making the phone call.

"Let's sleep on the porch," Jill suggested. "We can each have a couch by the windows and look out at the moon."

Nana agreed and brought soft flannel blankets and down pillows onto the porch, that overlooked the channel. "Don't turn on the lights if you want to watch the moon," she reminded them. "We must pull down the shades if the lights are turned on."

Jill loaned Wendy a pair of pajamas. "They're not fancy," she said apologetically. "I need more clothes. I just didn't want to bring too much on the train."

"I would have thought you'd have scads of clothes, having a dad who's a famous entertainer," said Wendy.

"We're just ordinary people," Jill said defensively. "My dad sings for a living. He makes records and sings on the radio and at nightclubs. It's his job, Wendy. Besides, I *do* have nice clothes. I just didn't bring my whole wardrobe!"

Wendy looked flustered, then nodded. "I'm sorry, Jill. Actually, I don't have a lot of clothes myself. Maybe I'll shop at Bayswater too. My aunt Adrie will give me the money. She loves to buy me things."

Jill didn't answer. Wendy must have a steamer trunk to carry all the clothes she brought, she thought.

After the girls had changed and snuggled

down under their blankets, Wendy asked, "So, what do you think of Quarry?"

"He repeats too much stupid gossip."

"He has such a funny way of talking. Did you hear what he called my aunt Adrie? A tiptoe Nancy? What a nerve!"

"They all talk that way up *heah!*" Jill said. Both girls burst into giggles. "People tease *me* about my *Boston* accent," Jill continued. "But what makes me really mad is to hear Quarry repeat rumors about Nana."

"What about Quarry?" Nana came out to the porch and sat in a wicker rocking chair. "He seemed a bit upset when he left."

"Quarry says dumb things," Jill blurted. She pulled herself up onto one elbow. "Nana, Quarry says you and your Sunday-night group keep your get-togethers a secret and that has everyone wondering what's going on."

"It's no one's business," Wendy piped up.

"That's true," said Nana. "Well, to satisfy you girls I'll tell you this much. There are four of us: Jessie Tompson, Bertha Judge, Ida Wilmar, and me. We usually meet at Ida's house, but sometimes we meet at Jessie's. Jessie has a wonderful garden and greenhouse where we often have tea. You see, none of us are really Maine people. We're from away, as they say. If you're not a native, it's hard to become part of the community."

"Quarry said Mrs. Wilmar is German," Wendy told her.

"Oh dear, nothing gets by Quarry or anyone else in this town." Nana sighed. "Ida *is* German, and because of that some folks are suspicious of her. She's a lovely, quiet woman who came to this country with her husband many years ago. They were teachers in the Boston area. During the First World War, they taught people in our government—probably intelligence people—how to speak German."

"You mean they actually taught secret agents?" Wendy asked.

"Yes, and if the United States Government hired Ida to teach government officials, there's no reason in the world anyone should feel she's some sort of national threat. It's ridiculous!" Nana rocked harder in the chair.

"Where is Mrs. Wilmar's husband?" Jill asked.

"Now that *is* a mystery, and probably adds to the gossip. A while back, Mr. Wilmar's brother died. Mr. Wilmar went back to Germany to bring his brother's family over here. When this war broke out in Europe, though, the German government wouldn't let him come back. He's an elderly man now and Ida worries about him. She never hears from him anymore."

"That's terrible," said Jill.

"You'd think people would be kind to her, instead of being so cold," Nana said crossly. "Of course, not everyone in town is unkind. But it only takes a few to cause trouble."

"Lots of bad things are happening because of the war," Wendy said. "*C'est la guerre.* It's the war, as they say."

Nana got up. "Now, don't you girls believe all the stories you'll be hearing around town." She started for the living room. "Oh, and don't be too hard on Quarry. He's a good boy."

"He talks too much," said Jill.

"He puts both his big feet in his mouth," Wendy added.

Nana chuckled. "Good night, girls."

As Jill and Wendy discussed what they would wear to the clambake on Saturday, the full moon drifted behind gathering clouds. The western summer breeze shifted to a stiffening easterly wind that rattled the shutters. Soon a driving rain splattered against the windows of the porch.

"I hope it doesn't rain on Saturday," Jill whispered sleepily.

"Saturday is six days away," Wendy said. "Don't forget your dare, Jill, about getting us into the Crystals. I'm sure those girls will be at the clambake. We'll get Quarry to introduce us to them then."

Jill rolled over and buried her head in the down pillow. "Oh, all right," she groaned, just before falling asleep.

Although the rain had stopped on Monday morning, a bleak sea fog shrouded everything and a foghorn moaned cheerlessly over the still air.

"I can't even see the ocean," Jill said peering through the windowpane. "We're fogged in."

"It will burn off," Wendy said with a yawn.

The aroma of bacon drifted from the kitchen.

"Breakfast is almost ready!" Nana called.

The girls dressed quickly and went to the kitchen, where Nana had set the table with a bright red tablecloth and Fiesta dishes of every color.

"This looks so cheery," Wendy exclaimed. "And bacon! You're wasting your meat coupons on me!"

"It's not *wasted*," Nana chided her. "It's a treat for us to have you with us for breakfast." She reached for the girls' hands and bowed her head. Wendy looked a little startled, then bowed her head too.

After saying grace, Nana said, "Help yourself, girls," and handed Wendy a yellow platter of fresh eggs and bacon.

"Thank you so much," said Wendy, scooping food onto her plate.

After they finished breakfast, Jill looked out the window. "The fog is lifting. Everything has a golden, misty look." The sea was picking up flickers of sun. Jill could now make out the shape of the lighthouse across the channel.

"I should probably get back to help Aunt

Adrie," said Wendy. "She said guests may start coming any day now for the holiday."

"I'll take you back *over to home* now. That's how they say it up here." Nana laughed and took her car keys from a hook over the sink. "Do you want to come, Jill?"

"No, I'll wait *heah*," Jill answered with a grin at Wendy.

"Jill, you'll be a native in no time 'tall." Nana headed out the back door. "Wendy, get your things together, dear, and come out to the garage. I'll be waiting in the car."

"I'll see you soon," said Wendy before she left. "Don't forget your dare! We're going to get into the Crystals somehow, someway."

"I don't know why it's so important to you."

"Come on, Jill," Wendy coaxed. "It would be nice to be included with the girls here. After all, we'll be in Winter Haven all summer."

"Okay, okay. I'll try."

Nana was backing out of the garage. "Bye," Wendy called as she headed toward the car. "Buzz me."

"I will." Jill waved good-bye from the door and

watched the car disappear down the road and around the bend.

She was clearing the table when she heard scuffling sounds. "What's that racket?" She went to the back door and peered out. "Oh my goodness! Sarge! No!"

Sarge was sprawled on the floor of the porch. In his clutch was a shivering bundle of brown-and-white feathers.

Jill ran out. "Shoo, bad cat!" she yelled. "Sarge! Let go of that bird!" Sarge's ears went flat and he clamped a paw even tighter across the wriggling bird. "Oh, it's a pigeon! The poor thing!" As she approached Sarge, he tried to drag the bird away. "Scat!" Jill yelled.

Sarge reluctantly let go of his prize and slunk off the porch.

"Oh, you poor little thing," Jill crooned as she bent over the wounded pigeon and smoothed its feathers. "What's this?" A tiny metal cylinder was attached to the bird's right leg. Jill gasped in surprise. This was a carrier pigeon! Where did it come from? And where was it going?

Jill could feel the bird's heart beating rapidly

as she picked it up and carried it into the kitchen. She lay the bird on a tea towel. Then, taking a pair of pliers, she gently pried off the leg band.

The bird wriggled and fluttered as Jill pulled at the canister latches with her thumbnail and popped open the minuscule container.

A tiny slip of paper was rolled up inside. Jill pulled it out and opened it carefully.

Scribbled in ink were the words *Sonnabend iv.*

10

The Three Wise Monkeys

Jill rolled the scrap of paper, stuffed it back into the cylinder, then tucked it in her pocket. What do the words *Sonnabend iv* mean? she wondered. And why had the bird come *here*?

The bird struggled to fly but only seemed able to flutter. Jill couldn't find a broken wing or any blood. "You're not hurt badly," she said. "I think you're just stunned." She found an empty carton in the pantry, held the pigeon in it with one hand, and carried the box out to the garage.

"You'll be safe here," she whispered as she placed the box on a workbench. She found some birdseed in a canvas satchel and sprinkled it in the box. Then she brought a dish of water from the house. "I'll check on you every day," she promised the shivering bird. "And I'll make sure the doors are shut so Sarge can't get in."

Jill closed the garage, then sat on the porch steps and opened up the capsule again. *Sonnabend iv.* Perhaps the bird was part of a racing team. Homing pigeon races were a popular sport.

Still, there was a war going on. Weren't carrier pigeons used during wars to carry secret messages? Maybe she should tell someone. She shook her head. No. Certainly no one in Winter Haven would know anything about secret messages. This was probably a racing bird.

Yet the word *Sonnabend* wasn't English. Could it be a German word? Could someone in Winter Haven be a German sympathizer? Wait a second! What if someone knew Jill had found the message? And what about all the rumors Quarry had told her about Nana? If anyone even suspected a carrier pigeon had come here, there would be even more talk. No, she wouldn't tell anyone. Not even Nana. Not yet, anyway. She'd just say that Sarge had hurt a pigeon and she put it in the garage to see if it would live.

At that very moment, Nana's car came up the driveway. "Sarge caught a bird. It's hurt, so I put it in a box in the garage," Jill explained through the driver's-side window. "That's why the door is shut."

"So the great hunter has struck again. What kind of bird this time?"

"A pigeon."

"Poor thing!" Nana got out of the car, carrying a small parcel. "Surprise for Miss Jill Winters!" she said, handing the package to Jill. "This came special delivery. I saw Joe Downs, the mailman, on his route and he stopped to give it to me. I think it's from your father."

Jill smiled as she recognized her father's neat handwriting. The return address was the Balboa Hotel in Los Angeles. Dad sent her a gift all the way from California! She ripped off the brown wrapping paper to reveal a narrow white jewelry box. Jill held her breath as she opened it. A gold bracelet shimmered in the sunlight. "Look, Nana! It's a charm bracelet with—three monkeys!"

"There's a card," Nana said.

Jill read it out loud. "'I know what a little worry-wart you can be, so I'm sending you the three wise monkeys! They know just what to do about worries. Love, Daddy.' What does he mean, Nana?"

Nana held up the bracelet. "See? This monkey is covering its eyes with its hands. That means 'see no evil.' This one's covering its ears. That means 'hear no evil.' And the third one here is covering his mouth 'speak no evil.'" Nana fastened the bracelet around Jill's wrist. "These monkeys *are* wise. They'll remind you not to listen to gossip or repeat rumors or imagine things that might worry you."

The monkeys jingled on Jill's wrist. She was glad she'd decided to say nothing about the pigeon's curious message that was tucked deep down in her pocket. She wouldn't repeat her own uncertainties. *Speak no evil.*

Back in the kitchen, Jill cleared the table and poured hot water into the dishpan. Nana wiped the dishes as Jill washed. "Nana, did you ever hear of the Crystals? Wendy wants to join."

"It's part of a social club. I believe some parents started it several years ago. They wanted their children to mingle with the *better* families."

"What do you mean?"

"Well, they're probably the bankers and the doctors and lawyers in the area. I don't believe the children of farmers or fishermen are included. It's rather snobbish, in my opinion. Are you sure you want to join?"

"No, but Wendy does."

Nana wiped off the counter. "I hope she doesn't get turned down. She might be hurt."

"She wants *me* to try to get into the Crystals first." Jill folded the dish cloth and hung it on a rack. "Wendy said they'll let me join because my dad is Drew Winters."

Nana sat down at the table. "When I first moved here I was asked to join the local women's club, but not until they found out Drew Winters is my son."

"Did you join?"

"No, and I'm sure that I insulted them. They've never been too friendly since then. But I don't care to spend time with those ladies and their functions. I'd rather just be here and paint the beautiful scenery and . . ."

"And meet on Sundays with your friends," Jill finished.

"That's right. I choose to be with friends who like me for who I am—not because my son is a well-known entertainer." Nana got up and looked out the window. "The light is beautiful now—all diffused and golden. This is why I love it here."

Jill joined her and gazed out at the distant point. The lighthouse had caught the morning sun and reminded her of a silent angel guarding the harbor. At night it became a white candle that cast a comforting glow.

"I think I'll set up my easel out on the rocks and do some painting. The lighthouse is a perfect subject. Would you like to give it a try?"

"No thank you, Nana. I'm not so good at painting. I'll write a letter to Dad to thank him for the bracelet."

Nana gathered the easel and folding chair which she kept near the porch door. "Jill, would you carry the portfolio and paints for me?" She pointed to a leather satchel. Together they headed across the damp grass to the point. A soft breeze played with the waves and the sea glittered as if bits of mirrors had been scattered across the surface.

After setting up the easel and chair for Nana, Jill was heading back to the house when she heard her name.

"Hey, Jill!" Quarry was riding up the driveway.

"What are you doing here?" Jill felt a little guilty when she saw Quarry's smile fade. After all, he did apologize last night. She ran to the driveway. "Want to come in?"

Quarry grinned again and nodded, then leaned his bicycle against the side of the garage.

Once inside the kitchen Quarry said, "Jill, I wanted to say"—he shifted from one foot to the other—"I'm awful sorry I aggravated you last night. Those rumors I repeated are just a lotta chalk and water."

"I'm sorry I got so mad," Jill said. "Come on out to the sunporch."

They sat on the window seat facing each other. "I just got a job," Quarry told her. "I'm gonna be workin' at Guy Binette's grocery store every mornin' until noon—startin' tomorrow. He needs help and I can use the money."

"I met him yesterday. He had just put up a flag with the single star in the window."

"Guy worries a lot about Paulie. He says it cheers him up to have me there." Quarry cleared his throat. "So are you goin' to the clambake on Saturday?"

"Yes. I wouldn't miss a real Maine clambake."

Quarry shifted in his seat. "Jill, would you like to go to the clambake with me?"

Jill was taken by surprise. She thought Quarry liked Wendy. "You mean . . . on a date?"

"Well, sort of. We'd ride our bikes to the clambake together and stick with each other while we're there. Then we'd come home together."

"Um. Okay, I guess so. I had planned to go with Wendy . . ." Jill noticed a look of disappointment cross Quarry's face. "I'll just tell her we'll meet her there," she said quickly. "Thanks for inviting me, Quarry. I've got a problem, though. My bike has a flat."

"I'll fix it for you right now," said Quarry, standing up. "Is it in the garage?"

"Yes, come on." Jill led Quarry into the garage through the side door.

"By Godfrey! Wha—what's that?" he yelled as the pigeon fluttered erratically over their heads.

Jill laughed. "I forgot to warn you about the pigeon." The bird flopped onto the workbench. "Close the door." Quarry looked puzzled but did as Jill asked. "Sarge caught the pigeon this morning. I thought I'd keep him in here until he's well enough to fly." She pointed to the bicycle. "There it is, flat tire and all."

Quarry gathered some tools and a tube of tire patches that he found on the workbench. "Let's take the bike outside where it's light," he said, handing the tools to Jill. "I'll get the bike and you hold the door so your bird don't fly away."

He sat on the grass by the driveway and removed the bicycle wheel, then pulled the deflated tube from the tire. "Have you heard from your mother yet?"

"No, but I'm trying not to worry."

Quarry nodded, concentrating on the patched-up tube. After a moment, he looked at Jill. "I hear a lot about what's goin' on out there on the sea 'cause of Pa keepin' the light and all." He looked apologetic. "My pa'd make a touse if he knew I was listenin' to his calls. And he'd be even madder if he knew I told anyone."

Jill fingered the charms on her bracelet. "Have you heard something about ships in Newfoundland?"

"Oh, no!" Quarry said hastily. "See? I always say the wrong thing. I just wanted you to know why words pop from my mouth like they do."

"I guess words pop out of my mouth too," Jill said. "I'm sorry I get upset so easily, but I do worry about my mother, my dad, and my sick uncle, too. I wish I knew how he is, and I wish I could speak to my mother."

"It's hard when you don't know what's goin' on," Quarry admitted. "Don't believe everything you hear. Most war rumors are a little noth o' noth . . ."

"Noth o' noth?" Jill interrupted.

"You know. There ain't nothin' *north of north,*" Quarry explained. "Means you shouldn't pay any 'tention."

Jill wondered if Quarry had heard anything about carrier pigeons. Should she tell him about the bird and the message? Quarry knew a lot. But he talked a lot too.

Quarry was watching her. "What is it?"

"Nothing . . . er . . . I was just thinking about . . . carrier pigeons. Do you know anything about them?"

"I know they're used by the government to carry messages where they can't get through any other way."

"Has your dad ever mentioned them? I mean . . . are there any around here?"

"Not that I know of." Quarry looked at her warily. "Why? Is that bird in there a carrier pigeon?"

"Quarry, it had a message attached to its leg." Jill blurted out her secret.

"Good Godfrey!" He stood up. "Are you kiddin' me?"

"No. It's the truth."

"What did the message say? Where is it?"

"In my pocket." Jill's face felt suddenly hot. What was she doing?

"Show me!"

It was too late to unsay the words. Now she had to trust Quarry. "If I show it to you, you must *swear* you won't tell anyone. Not your dad. Not *anyone*. You've got to *promise*!"

"But, Jill, this might have to do with war secrets or spies or somethin'. I can't make that promise."

"I don't mean you can't tell *ever*. I don't want to tell anyone *yet*. This bird came to *our* house and you know all the stupid talk about Nana and Ida Wilmar. I want to find out more myself, first," Jill pleaded. "Besides, who can we trust? If this is a secret message we might get in trouble. Then what?"

"I hadn't thought of that." Quarry looked troubled. "Okay, Jill. You're probably right. We've gotta be real careful. Now, show me the message that the bird was carryin'."

"Not until you *swear* you'll keep this a secret."

Quarry put up his hand, the same way Jill had the night before. "I swear, Jill. I won't tell anyone. I'll die first!"

Jill pulled the tiny container from her pocket, clicked it open, and handed Quarry the scrap of paper. "Here, read it."

"*Sonnabend iv.*" He scratched his head. "What does that mean?"

"I don't know. Do you suppose it's a German

word?" Jill's voice rose. "I'm scared. I probably shouldn't have opened the capsule."

"Of course you had to open it. Don't worry, Jill, we'll find out what it's all about." He looked at Jill's bracelet. "Hey, what's this?"

"My dad sent it to me." She pointed to each of the monkeys. "See no evil; hear no evil; speak no evil."

"That's right cunnin'. Yep, it's somethin' for me to remember too." Quarry took a deep breath. "Okay, first of all, we need to find out what the word *Sonnabend* means. Wendy's aunt speaks lots of different languages. Maybe she could help."

"No, we can't tell *anyone*! Not Wendy. Not Adrie. Not *anyone*! You promised!"

"Okay, Jill. Okay. We'll find some other way."

They were both silent for a few moments, then Jill remembered something. "Quarry, how stupid of me! My grandmother doesn't keep pigeons! So the bird wasn't heading home to *this* house. But that Clayton Bishop up the street has a pigeon coop!"

"That's right! Homin' pigeons only go *home*!" Quarry slapped his head. "What a buffle brain! I didn't think o' that neither."

"We can't trace who sent it, but once the bird is well, we can let it go from the widow's walk. We'll watch where it goes. It should fly right to the person who was intended to get this message!"

11

Made in Germany

"Clayton Bishop raises pigeons, but he says they're for food. Do you know anyone else in town who has pigeons?" Jill asked Quarry.

"No. I didn't even know Clayton Bishop had 'em. He's new around these heah parts."

"I'd love to set the bird free right now to see where it goes," Jill said. "It's probably well enough to fly. But I'd like to be sure it's healthy, so I think we should wait a few days."

"What'll we do with the message when we set it free?" Quarry asked. "If we attach the capsule to the bird, we may be helpin' the wrong guys. If we

don't send the message back with the bird, someone will know the pigeon was intercepted."

"We won't do anything yet," Jill said. "In the
meantime, we can find a German dictionary and
look up that word."

"I got an idea," Quarry said. "How 'bout us
sneakin' into Clayton's yard and seein' if any of
those pigeons have bands on 'em."

Jill frowned. "No Quarry, if he's involved and
finds us snooping around, who knows what he
might do. Besides, I didn't notice any bands on
the birds when I was there."

"You can go up to the widow's walk every day
and watch where he's goin' and who goes to his
house," Quarry suggested.

"I can spy on everyone from up there! If anyone is up to something bad in this town we'll flush
them out."

"Jill, this could be dangerous."

"I know. I can understand if you're scared,
Quarry."

"I ain't scared. But we might be stirrin' up a
hornet's nest . . ."

"Well, I *am* frightened. But I intend to find

out what's going on even if I have to do it by
myself! It's my patriotic duty! Now, are you going
to help me or not?"

Quarry gritted his teeth. "Okay. I'll come over
afternoons when I'm done at the grocery." Pa owns
some mighty strong binoculars. You can spot a flea
on a field mouse with 'em. He'll loan me a pair."

"Don't you *dare* tell him why," Jill cautioned.
"Remember your promise."

"I'll tell him we're bird-watchin'. And that's
the truth!"

"Who's bird-watching?" Nana had come back
from painting.

How much had she heard? "We thought it
might be fun to watch birds from the widow's
walk," Jill said quickly. "Do you think we could
see those cute little birds that look like clowns?"

"Oh, you mean puffins? You might be able to
spot them on the sides of cliffs if you have strong
binoculars. I may have some good field glasses in
the house somewhere."

"That's swell, Nana! It'll be such fun to list all
the birds we can spot. Oh, by the way, Quarry is
taking me to the clambake on Saturday."

"Sounds to me like you've made a lot of plans." Nana smiled at Quarry. "Now you go on up to the widow's walk while I search for those glasses."

After Nana went into the house, Quarry picked up the inner tube and put it into his bicycle basket. "This inner tube ain't no good. Too many patches. I'll try to get one at Guy's store tomorrow. They're hard to find with the rubber shortage and all."

"Thanks, Quarry."

"Do you want to go up to the lookout now?"

Jill nodded. "Let's go."

Inside the house, Nana was at a desk in the parlor. "I found the binoculars," she said, handing them to Jill. "Take those folding chairs up with you, Quarry." She pointed to wooden chairs with striped canvas seats, next to the closet door.

"Your grandmother's nice," Quarry said as they settled themselves in the chairs on the widow's walk.

Jill put the binoculars to her eyes and adjusted them. "These are swell! I can see right into Mr. Binette's grocery store!"

"You can watch me workin' every mornin' when you're up here. Let me try 'em." Quarry took the binoculars and gazed out to sea through the heavy lenses. "Aha!" he said dramatically. "Hey, there's a fillieloo flyin' around."

"A what?"

"Don't get to see many fillieloos in these heah parts," Quarry said.

"Let me see!" Jill reached for the glasses but stopped when Quarry laughed. "What is a fillieloo? You're poking fun at me."

Quarry grinned and nodded. "A fillieloo's a make-believe bird that flies backwards to keep the wind out of his face. We tell the summercater bird-watchers to be sure to watch for the fillieloo." He handed the binoculars back to Jill, who looked them over.

"Hey, look." Jill pointed to some engraved words on the barrel. "'Zeiss. Made in Germany.'" Where did Nana get these field glasses?

"Zeiss binoculars are probably the best in the world. You can't get 'em anywhere since the war. German products are off the markets."

"How do you know so much about it?"

"'Cause my pa talks about lenses all the time. The lighthouse uses big lenses to magnify the light it sends out. I've heard him mention Zeiss lenses dozens o' times. They're a German company that makes cameras and binoculars and telescopes — and stuff like that."

"How did Nana get these if they're not for sale in our country?"

"Maybe she got 'em before the war."

"But these look brand-new."

Quarry looked through the glasses again. "There's that Bishop guy, now. He's drivin' off in that old car of his."

"Let me see." Jill took the glasses and watched the car zoom down the road in a cloud of dust. She could see Clayton Bishop turn into town and park at Mr. Binette's store. "He's at the grocery store. Let's keep a record of everywhere he goes."

"You're not suspectin' Guy Binette of being a spy, are you?" Quarry raised his eyebrows skeptically. "Just 'cause Clayton Bishop is buyin' groceries at his store."

"I'm not suspecting anyone! *Yet.*" Jill glanced across the channel at the lighthouse and the rugged house where Quarry lived. "Maybe we should set up some way of sending messages to each other at night."

Quarry burst out laughing. "Just use the telephone, for cryin' out loud."

Jill flushed. "I suppose. But there may be an emergency sometime. And we *do* want to keep all this a secret."

"Okay. If ever anything is wrong, signal to me from the widow's walk with a flashlight. I'll know it's you—if I happen to be lookin' this way, that is." Quarry chuckled again.

"What's so funny? I'm beginning to think you believe this whole spy thing is stupid."

"Don't get riled up. I'm just teasin'. I've got to go over to home now, but I'll stop by the library on the way to see if I can find what that word *sonnabend* means. You stay here and keep an eye on Clayton Bishop."

"I'd go to the library with you, but I have no tire on my bike."

"I'll get it fixed today," Quarry promised.

"Quarry, don't ask for a German dictionary at the library. You'll have to look for it yourself."

"Stop worryin'. I'll keep my mouth as tight as a clam."

"You'd better," Jill warned. "If anyone finds out what we're doing, we could be in real trouble."

12

Invitations

Jill stayed up on the widow's walk and watched Quarry ride to town. He turned once to wave, and she waved back. She could see him through the binoculars as he parked his bicycle and started up the steps to the library, but then trees got in the way of her vision so she aimed the glasses at the grocery store. Clayton Bishop's car was gone. "Where did it go?" Jill sputtered. "I only took my eyes off of it for a few minutes. Darn!"

"Something wrong? Didn't you see any puffins?" Nana poked her head through the hatch and climbed up.

"No, I didn't see what I was looking for," Jill answered truthfully, "but I'm going to keep watching every day."

"I'm so glad you found a nice hobby. Jill, I noticed Quarry's gone, so I wondered if we should go to Bayswater now instead of waiting until tomorrow."

"That would be fun! I'll buzz Wendy and see if she can come. I hope she doesn't have to work."

"I'm sure . . . Adrie can get along without her for a few hours." Nana frowned. "Coming from the city, I still find it so awkward to call everyone by first names. I suppose it's less formal and more friendly."

"People aren't that friendly here—even with the first names. Quarry thinks Adrie is *icebound*— that she's real cold to people."

"She does seem rather moody," Nana agreed, "but she surely loves Wendy."

Jill headed down the stairs to place the telephone call and change into her slacks suit. She removed the binoculars from around her neck. "Nana, where did you get these binoculars?"

"I don't remember. They were your grand-

father's." Nana descended the steep stairway
behind Jill, sealing the hatch behind her.

Wendy was standing on the sidewalk when Jill
and Nana drove up. "Thanks a million for inviting
me," she said as she climbed into the backseat of
the car. "Oh, Aunt Adrie would like you both to
stay for supper when we get back. She has something special on the menu. And she has a new
chef, too. He's a foreigner. He doesn't speak
English. But he sure can cook!"

"Where's he from?" Jill asked.

"Spain, I think," Wendy said. "His name is
Max."

"Max? That doesn't sound Spanish. Maybe
he's French. There are a lot of French Canadians
in this part of Maine," Nana suggested. "But on
second thought, Max doesn't sound like a French
name, either."

On the half-hour drive to Bayswater, Jill and
Wendy sang some of the latest songs on the hit
parade. "Don't Sit Under the Apple Tree" and
"Tangerine."

"You have a nice voice," Wendy said. "You must take after your father."

"No one can compare to my dad," Jill responded. "But thanks for the compliment. What's your favorite popular song, Wendy?" she asked. "Mine is 'I Hear a Rhapsody.'"

"Doesn't Drew have that on one of his records?" Nana asked.

"Yes," Jill answered. "It's beautiful."

"That's my favorite too," Wendy said. "It's been number one on the hit parade for ten weeks."

"What's your favorite, Nana?"

"'I'll Be Seeing You,'" she answered. "But war songs make me cry."

"I wonder what songs Daddy will sing on *Manhattan Merry-Go-Round* Sunday night," Jill said.

"I'm coming over to listen with you. That'll be so exciting. Quarry said he'd come too." Wendy leaned over the back of Jill's seat and whispered, "I'm pretty sure he likes me."

Jill knew she'd have to tell Wendy that Quarry

had invited *her* to the clambake, but now was not the right time.

At Bayswater, Nana found a parking space in front of Miller's Department Store. A sign in the window read NEWEST FASHIONS FROM BOSTON AND NEW YORK. Mannequins in slacks suits with heavily padded shoulders stood stiffly in the show windows. The newest fad, shoulder-strap purses, like those worn by the Women's Army Corps, hung from their arms.

"You're right up-to-date," Wendy said, pointing to Jill's slacks. "All you need is one of those purses."

Jill hoped Wendy hadn't noticed the small repair Nana had made in the knee of her trousers.

The first floor of the store had counters featuring makeup and perfumes. While Nana looked for some night cream for her face, Wendy found a display of sample bottles and began splashing various scents on her wrists. "Mmm, this one is so flowery. It reminds me of Aunt Adrie's favorite French perfume." She shoved her wrist under Jill's nose.

Jill spotted a golden bottle of Tweed. "This is my mom's favorite. She squeezed the atomizer, spraying the refreshing fragrance over her neck. With the familiar tangy scent, a sadness and longing for her mother swept over Jill.

"Come on!" Wendy pulled Jill toward the escalator. After making her purchase, Nana followed them.

Wendy pointed to the sign that read JUNIOR DEB DEPARTMENT. "I like this place. They refer to us as 'junior debs.' I hate it when they call us 'bobby-soxers.' It sounds so juvenile."

Wendy held up a scoop-necked peasant-style blouse and admired herself in a mirror. "Aunt Adrie gave me twenty dollars to spend on anything I want." She pulled a flowered skirt from the rack and headed for the dressing room. "I'm going to try these on."

"*Twenty dollars!*" Nana whispered. "Her aunt is so generous with her."

"I want to try a peasant outfit too," Jill said, "but now she'll think I'm copying her."

"If you see something you like, get it. Don't worry about Wendy."

"What would be the right thing to wear to a clambake?" Jill asked.

Nana picked out a pair of white cotton pants with blue-and-white-striped cuffs. "These are cute. And they're called clam diggers. See? They're longer than shorts, but shorter than slacks. Perfect for a clambake." She reached for a halter type of top. "Look at this, Jill. One half is red-and-white stripes, and the other blue and white. It matches the pants and it's just the right colors for the Fourth of July!"

"Can I try them on?" Jill asked. "Would Daddy let me wear something like this?"

"Well, he'd better, or he'll have to answer to me, because I think they're just fine," Nana said firmly.

Jill beamed at her grandmother and took the outfit to the dressing room. She changed quickly and stepped out to the three-way mirror. Wendy was already there, turning and posing in the peasant outfit. A few women stopped to watch her. Wendy could be a model, Jill thought enviously.

"I'll take this," Wendy said to the saleslady who stood nearby.

Jill took her turn in front the mirror. She looked taller and rather glamorous in the pants and halter. And to think Nana picked this out! It was perfect for a sunny day at the ocean.

Jill could see Wendy in the reflection, looking her up and down. "Are you wearing that to the clambake?"

"I think so," Jill answered.

Wendy shrugged and went back into the dressing room.

Jill ended up with the clam digger outfit, a short set, a bathing suit, and a terry-cloth beach robe — plus a pair of white canvas shoes. Canvas shoes with rope soles had become popular since leather was being reserved for servicemen. She and Wendy piled their packages into the trunk of the car, then Nana said, "Let's go for an ice cream before heading home."

The Palace of Sweets was just up the street. White wrought-iron tables and chairs were clustered on the sidewalk and inside the dining area. Behind the counter a girl in a peppermint-striped uniform made sodas for a group of girls sitting on tall stools.

Jill, Wendy, and Nana found an empty table and ordered sundaes. Jill could see the other girls watching them from the mirror behind the counter. A dark-haired girl cupped her hand over her mouth and whispered something to the others. Jill recognized her from the gesture. They were the ones who had snubbed her on the library steps.

After a moment of discussion, the three girls slipped off their stools and headed toward Jill's table.

"Hi," said the dark-haired girl. "How are you, Elizabeth? Remember me? I'm Elaine O'Brien. I think you know my mother. She's the president of the Women's Club."

"Oh yes, of course," said Nana.

"And these are my friends Gloria Brandt and Betty Whitfield."

"Nice to meet you," Nana said. "This is my granddaughter, Jill, and this is Wendy Taylor."

"Oh yes, Adrie Dekker's niece," said Elaine. Jill noticed Elaine nudged Betty very slightly. "So you're Drew Winters's daughter," Elaine said to Jill. "We have all his records."

Jill nodded, and was relieved when the waitress brought the sundaes to their table. She picked up her long spoon and began to scoop the whipped cream and hot fudge.

"Is your father coming up to Winter Haven this summer?" Gloria asked.

"Probably, when he's through with his tour," Jill mumbled with her mouth full.

"I hear tell he's going to be singing on the radio Sunday night," Elaine said.

"Where did you hear that?" Jill asked.

Betty spoke up. "Quarry MacDonald told us."

There goes Quarry with his big mouth, Jill thought.

"My dad's in the movie business," Wendy said. Then she looked at Jill and flushed. "I mean he owns a big movie theater in New York."

"Jill, we belong to a very exclusive club called the Crystals. We'd love to have you come visit us tomorrow night for a tea," said Elaine.

"Then, if everything goes well, we'll invite you to join us," Betty explained. "It'd be wonderful to have Drew Winters's daughter as a member of our crowd. Will you come?"

Jill could see Wendy's pleading look. "I suppose I could come, but I'd like to bring Wendy along too."

The three girls gazed at Wendy as if debating, then Elaine said, "Well, sure. That would be swell."

"Oh, I can't wait!" Wendy said. "It would be so nice to be part of . . . well, I've heard so much about the Crystals, I can't believe I'll finally get to . . ."

Betty interrupted. "We'll have a tea at seven o'clock downstairs in the church hall."

"Is the Crystals a church organization?" Nana asked.

"No, but we're a charitable group and we do so many good things for the community that Reverend Bailey lets us use the hall for meetings. So you'll come, Jill?" Elaine asked.

"We'll be glad to," Wendy said eagerly. "It will be fun, won't it Jill? We'll *both* be there."

"Mmm, yes," Elaine murmured. She turned to Jill. "See you tomorrow."

"All right," Jill said. "Bye."

"Thank you!" Wendy called.

The girls walked off. Jill noticed that Elaine looked back once, then whispered something to her friends.

"I'm so thrilled! We've been invited to join the Crystals!" Wendy exclaimed.

"No, we haven't," Jill corrected her. "We've been invited to tea to pass inspection. Then we might *possibly* be invited to join the Crystals."

"Naturally we'll pass inspection," Wendy said, dipping into her melting sundae. "Why wouldn't we? After all, you're Drew Winters's daughter and I'm your best friend."

13

Supper at the Tearoom Inn

It was almost six o'clock when Nana parked the car near the inn.

"You're coming in, aren't you?" Wendy asked as she gathered up her shopping bags. "Aunt Adrie insists that you stay for supper. This is her official opening of the restaurant. People will start to come and take rooms for the big celebration on the Fourth—and then for the summer."

"Well, I don't want to disappoint Adrie, and it sounds like she's expecting us," Nana said.

Inside the tearoom, candles were flickering on the tables, which were set with white linen tablecloths and crystal glasses. "How pretty!" Jill exclaimed.

Adrie bustled in from another room to welcome them. "I'm so glad you're here," she said, taking Wendy's parcels and putting them in a nearby closet. "There's something special on the menu tonight. I don't want to tell—I want to surprise you." Adrie could be so friendly sometimes, and so snippy other times. Jill again noticed the resemblance to Wendy—that single mischievous dimple in their right cheeks that emerged when they smiled. Adrie led them to a table by the window and held the chair for Nana.

"Thank you, Adrie," Nana said, sitting down. "Just look at these carnations and baby's breath." Nana gestured to the red-and-white flowers in a slender vase.

"A friend knew I was opening officially today and sent me a basketful of flowers," said Adrie. "There were enough for every table."

"They're lovely, and they add so much to your decor," Nana said. "Who sent them?"

"I don't know. There was no card." Adrie

smiled. "The season is starting on a positive note, despite this blasted war. I also have a new cook. Max does magic with what little we can eat, considering the rationing and all." Adrie started back to the kitchen, then paused. "Wendy, will you give me a hand with the chowder?"

Wendy followed her aunt through a swinging door.

"There are only a few other people here," Nana whispered, looking around.

"Wendy says the inn will be full by this weekend."

"I don't know when I've seen Adrie so pleasant," Nana commented. "I think she enjoys having Wendy with her."

Jill looked out the windows at the boats on their moorings rising and falling in the swells, while a flock of gulls chased a fishing vessel to the docks. It was a nice way to end the day, and concerns about homing pigeons and secret messages seemed like a dream—but her worries about her mother were always close in her mind. Sabotage was another concern, since her father flew all over the country on airplanes. What if something happened to both of them? She fingered the monkey charms on her bracelet.

Wendy returned carrying a tray with three bowls of soup. She placed one at each setting then put the tray on another table. "New England clam chowder," she said. "A specialty of the house." She sat down, arranging a napkin on her lap. "Aunt Adrie says I should say that whenever I serve clam chowder," she whispered.

"Is this the surprise?" Jill asked.

"No, that's coming next. She showed me, but I'm not supposed to tell."

The chowder was delicious, chock-full of clams and potatoes and served with hard biscuits. After the soup dishes were removed, Adrie appeared with their supper. What looked like two tiny split chickens were arranged on each plate, with red currant jelly, watercress, and slices of lemon for garnish.

"Squab!" Adrie announced. "The most delicate, delicious food in the world." She leaned over to Nana and whispered, "And not one ration stamp needed!" She and Wendy served platters of mashed potatoes and fresh peas. Jill noticed how

Adrie's ruby ring glowed in the candlelight. What kind of a ruby was it? Hadn't Adrie called it a "rare pigeon's blood ruby"?

"Enjoy your meal," Adrie said as she returned to the kitchen.

"Such a fancy feast!" Nana held her hands poised over the squab, as if uncertain what to do with it.

Wendy daintily broke off one of the small legs and held it to her mouth. "It's okay to eat it this way," she said. "It's too small to slice. Besides, no one is watching."

Jill stared at the tiny birds on her plate and thought of the pigeon in the garage. She had no appetite for squab—or anything else—now. But when Nana gave her a slight frown, she stabbed one of the birds, plucked out the meat, and reluctantly ate it. It wasn't as sweet as chicken and had a slightly bitter taste. Jill gulped water to wash it down.

After a dessert of Boston cream pie, Jill and Nana got up to leave.

"Thanks for supper," Jill said to Wendy and Adrie.

"Yes, thank you," Nana said as she stepped outside. "It was delicious."

"I'm glad you enjoyed the squab," Adrie said. "I got it fresh from a gentleman who raises them for restaurants. You met him when you fell off your bicycle, Jill. Remember? I didn't know him at the time, but I've decided to order squab from him on a regular basis."

"I remember him only too well." Jill followed her grandmother to the sidewalk and got into the car.

Nana was about to step off the curb to get into the driver's seat, when someone called out, "Yoo-hoo! Elizabeth!"

"Hello, Ida!" Nana said. "Come meet my granddaughter."

Ida Wilmar lumbered toward them, puffing a little. She peeked into Jill's window. "My, my, so this is Jill. She looks much like you, Elizabeth." The woman's voice boomed and Jill detected a strong accent.

"How do you do," Jill said.

"Nice, thank you," Mrs. Wilmar said pleasantly. "I hope you'll come visit me some time while you're here, Liebchen." She turned back to Nana. "Now, Elizabeth, I need to ask you something about our next meeting. I understand . . ." At that moment a noisy truck drove by. Jill strained to hear but could not make out the conversation.

After the truck had passed, Jill heard Nana say, "Well if you feel that's the best way. We'll keep it a secret as usual."

Before Ida waved and walked away, Jill clearly recognized her last word to Nana.

"*Sonnabend!*"

14

The Kelpie

Jill's heart raced and her hands shook so badly that the monkeys on her bracelet jingled. *Sonnabend.* Jill couldn't keep silent another second. "Nana," she demanded, when her grandmother finally got into the car. "What were you talking about with Mrs. Wilmar?"

"We were just planning our next get-together," Nana said, starting the engine.

"What does *sonnabend* mean?"

Nana frowned. "Hmm, there's a funny sound in this engine. Do you hear it? I wonder if I should have the spark plugs cleaned. I'd hate to get stuck somewhere."

Jill sank back into the seat, shut her eyes, and didn't speak again all the way home. Nana was avoiding her question. That proved something was very wrong.

Back at the house, Jill helped Nana take the packages out of the car. Nana noticed Jill's silence and asked, "Don't you feel well?" Jill looked away but Nana gently turned her chin, forcing Jill to look into her eyes. "You're so quiet. Tell me what's wrong."

"You tell me, Nana!" Jill had to control her quivering voice. "You didn't answer me when I asked you before. What does *sonnabend* mean?"

"I must not have heard you." Nana looked puzzled. "Why, I don't know what it means. Where did you hear that word?"

"Ida Wilmar said it to you."

"Then it's probably German. I'll ask her, if you want me to."

"No, never mind." Jill felt close to tears.

"Why is it so important?"

"It's not important." Jill gathered up her parcels from Miller's and headed for the stairs. "I'm tired. I think I'll go to bed."

"You've had a busy day, Jill. I hope you feel better in the morning."

Jill paused on the stairs. "Thank you for the clothes. They'll be nice for the clambake."

"You're welcome." Nana looked perplexed and a little sad.

Jill closed her bedroom door and tossed the new clothes on a chair. She threw herself on the bed and gathered the pillow into her arms. She loved Nana, but what was going on between her and Ida Wilmar that was such a secret? Why wouldn't she answer when Jill questioned her about the word *sonnabend*?

She rubbed the three monkeys. Maybe her scary thoughts were her own doing—seeing and hearing evil. She'd had so many suspicions about Clayton Bishop, and now she found he really *did* raise squab. Hadn't she eaten them for supper herself? And Nana was the sweetest person on earth. She couldn't be involved in anything bad. Still, what secret did she share with Ida Wilmar?

Everything was all mixed-up. Jill cradled her head into the cool pillow. From her open window she could hear the waves crashing against the rocks as she fell into a fitful sleep.

In her dreams she was on the widow's walk. The wind whipped around her and clouds flew across the face of a full moon. Suddenly a wail came from the ocean. Jill fearfully turned her gaze to the dark waves and the shadows that rose and fell on the night sea.

A misty form took shape and sprang from the surf—a black horse, its mane tossing and tangling in the wind, its bloodred eyes blazing!

Slowly the horse dissolved into another black shadow. Adrie now stood on the waves smiling and beckoning to Jill—and glowing on her finger was her ruby ring.

Jill was startled from her sleep by a door opening. "Jill, your mother is on the telephone," Nana called. "Hurry now. Her time is limited."

Jill darted from her bed and ran to the hall telephone. "Mom! Mom! Where are you?"

"I'm in Grand Falls, Jill." Her voice was faint over the crackling of the wires. "Uncle Cliff died yesterday." There was a long pause, and Jill knew her mother was crying.

"Oh, Mom, I'm sorry," she said, tears springing to her own eyes.

"It's all right, Jill. I just needed to hear your voice. Once the funeral is over and things get straightened out here, I'll be coming back. I miss you so much." Her voice went loud and soft and was mixed with static.

"Mom, I wanted to tell you how sorry I am that I was so mean to you . . . I miss you! Please come home soon . . ." The noisy interference drowned out her voice.

The operator interrupted. "Your three minutes are up."

"Mom, did you hear me? Don't hang up!"

But the call had been disconnected.

Jill hung up the receiver and turned to her grandmother. "Nana, I was so mean to Mom before she left! I was mad 'cause she wouldn't take me with her." She tried not to cry. "I told her . . . she cared more about . . . Uncle Cliff than me!" Jill went to her grandmother's outstretched arms and buried her face in Nana's soft chenille bathrobe. "I wouldn't even throw her a kiss good-bye!"

"It's all right, dear," Nana crooned, rocking her. "I'm sure your mother understands."

"Suppose her ship was torpedoed and I could never tell her I was sorry . . ." Jill's tears were overflowing. "I'm so glad she called . . ." Jill stammered between sobs. "And I tried to tell her I was sorry . . . but the connection went bad. She never heard me." Jill looked up at Nana. "She was crying."

"She just lost her brother, Jill. But you're her guiding star and you can be sure she'll do everything to get back to you as soon as she can." Nana pulled a handkerchief from her pocket and wiped Jill's tears. After a while, Nana whispered. "Let's go have us a cup of tea."

Jill nodded and hugged her grandmother. How could she *ever* have had doubts about Nana and her friends?

In the kitchen Nana soon had the kettle singing and Jill began to feel better. She sipped tea and munched on molasses cookies. Then, noticing the clock, she exclaimed, "It's three in the morning. What time is it in Newfoundland?"

"Four-thirty. Your mother must have been able to get a ride out to Grand Falls, where there's a telephone. Then she would have had to wait her turn until she could get through to you. Remember? Sometimes it takes hours to get a long distance operator and connections, because of the war."

"Well, I'd stay up all night to talk to her. Oh, it was so good to hear her voice — even though she sounded far, far away."

After their tea, they each went back to bed, and Jill, wide awake now, began to think about her mother's trip home. Once more Mom would have to cross the Gulf through the waiting German submarines.

Jill recalled her dream. The kelpie had come to her tonight. The kelpie always warned of a coming disaster at sea!

15

Keep in the Sunlight

Jill slept fitfully until the midmorning sun drifted through the curtains. Sarge climbed onto her bed, purring and kneading the blanket. "I give up," she said. "I can't sleep around here!" She scratched Sarge's head and whispered, "Mom is coming home soon." She looked out the window and breathed in the salt air as she surveyed the morning sky and sea.

"That was just a silly dream about the kelpie last night," she told the cat. "Troubles always seem scarier at night."

She dressed quickly into comfortable shorts

and a shirt. Then she hung up her new clothes from Miller's.

Downstairs, Nana had a dish of blueberries and toast waiting for her. "How are you feeling this morning?" she asked. "Better?"

Jill nodded and slid into the chair. "I'm worried about Mom, Nana."

"Ben Franklin once said, 'Do not anticipate trouble or worry about what may never happen. Keep in the sunlight.' Did you know butterflies fly only on warm, sunny days?"

"No, I didn't know that."

"Have you ever seen one flying around on a rainy day? Think about it."

"I guess you're right, Nana. I never have."

"Everything will be all right in the big picture of things, Jill. Meanwhile, keep your thoughts in the sunlight where it's bright and promising, and you'll fly too."

"I worry about things too much, just like everyone says. I worried when I heard that German word Ida said to you."

Nana stood up. "I've been trying to remember what Ida might have said yesterday when you overheard that word. She and I were talking about changing the night of our next get-together to Saturday instead of Sunday. I'd like to be here with you on Sunday when your dad sings on the radio. That's what we were talking about, honey. You probably heard Ida say 'Saturday' in German."

Jill nodded. But what about keeping *the secret*? She distinctly remembered Nana saying something about "keeping it a secret as usual."

"Saturday is the clambake. Won't you be going?" Jill asked.

"I'll probably go straight to Ida's. Oh, Jill, I meant to tell you—Quarry's father came over early this morning and took your bike. He's going to fix it and bring it back later today."

"That's nice of him. Maybe I'll get a chance to meet him." Jill looked at the wall calendar. "Nana, tonight is the tea with the Crystals. I don't want to go, but I promised Wendy." She got up and went to the back door. "I'm going to check the pigeon and then do some bird-watching up on the widow's walk."

"I'll just stack the dishes in the sink and then go down to the point and paint."

When Jill opened the garage door, she frightened the bird, which flew around the shed and settled high on a beam. She poured fresh water into the dish, sprinkled seed over the workbench, then went up to the widow's walk.

Jill spent the morning on the lookout, scanning the town. She could see Quarry's bicycle in the rack outside Guy's grocery store. The binoculars were so strong that she could even zero in on the flag in the window—the one with the single star.

She aimed the glasses toward Clayton Bishop's house. His car was in the driveway, and the pump and pigeon coop were clearly visible. She was about to turn away when she noticed that Clayton had come out of the house carrying a basket and heading into the woods.

Jill watched Clayton until he disappeared into the trees. Then she aimed the binoculars beyond him—toward the rocky ledges that surrounded Frenchman's Cove. There was something out there on the water heading into the cove from the open sea. It was not much more than a shadow and she caught only a glimpse, because whatever it was moved out of sight behind the craggy cliffs.

Probably just some fishermen, Jill decided. She refused to let her imagination get out of control today.

That afternoon, Quarry came over with his father.

"Hello, Jill. Nice to meet you!" Hugh MacDonald shook her hand, then pulled Jill's and Quarry's bicycles out from the back of the truck. "I found an old inner tube in my shed that was hardly ever used. It fit slicker 'n a snail!"

"Thanks so much!" Jill exclaimed.

"Now you're all set to go to the clambake." Hugh winked at Quarry as he drove off.

"Did you get to the library?" Jill asked Quarry as soon as they were alone. "Did you find out what *Sonnabend* means?"

"Naw, the library was closed yesterday and won't open the rest of the week 'cause of the holiday."

"Quarry, I heard Ida Wilmar use that word last night! Would you believe it? So, I asked Nana if she knew what it meant. She thinks it means 'Saturday.'"

"Wait a minute." Quarry closed his eyes and

recited: "*Montag, Dienstag, Mittwoch, Donnerstag, Freitag, Samstag, Sonntag.*" He opened his eyes. "No, Saturday is *Samstag.*"

"You never said you spoke German!"

"I don't. I took a year of German in school and flunked. The only thing I remember are the days of the week."

"Never mind. At least we know it doesn't mean Saturday after all."

"We'll find out somehow," Quarry said. "Have you been up on the widow's walk? Have you been watchin' Clayton Bishop's house?"

"I saw Clayton walking out toward Frenchman's Cove this morning. I wonder if we have it all wrong, Quarry. Clayton *does* raise pigeons for food. I had two of them for supper last night at Adrie's."

"We may be crazier than outhouse rats to suspect anyone of anything!"

"Do you think we're imagining things?" Jill asked him.

"Maybe," Quarry replied.

"Maybe *not*," Jill insisted.

16

Tea with the Crystals

After supper Jill put on a flowered beige dress and a brown velveteen vest. "It looks a little wintry," she told Nana, "but it'll do."

"Your outfit looks wonderful with your brown hair and honey eyes," Nana replied.

Jill also wore rayon stockings and black patent-leather shoes with semi-high heels that Mom had bought before leather was rationed and which weren't quite broken in. She carried a matching black patent-leather bag.

Nana drove Jill to Wendy's. "You can walk to the church from here and ring me when you're done with the Crystals," she said after dropping her off.

Wendy bounced to the door in her new peasant skirt and blouse. An aqua ribbon was tied in her shining blond hair. Jill was astonished to see Wendy wearing another pair of expensive silk stockings with her multicolored sandals. "Where do you get real silk stockings?" she asked.

"Adrie gives them to me. Besides, she wants me to make a good impression on the Crystals," Wendy said. "I'm so excited!"

Adrie came to the door, her face drawn up in a troubled frown. "I'm not sure this is such a good idea, Jill. Those girls can be catty and I'd hate to see Wendy get hurt."

"I don't really want to join, but . . . ," Jill began.

Wendy interrupted her. "Oh, don't worry! We'll get into the Crystals, Aunt Adrie. They're *dying* for us to join."

"Well, good luck, then." Wendy's aunt watched them anxiously, then closed the door behind her.

As they strolled up Main Street, Wendy

paused to look at her reflection in almost every store window, straightening her hair ribbon or adjusting the neckline on her blouse. "Do I look all right?" she asked before they went into the church hall.

"You look beautiful," Jill said honestly. "You always do."

They entered a large room where tables and chairs had been set up. A group of about thirty girls had already arrived and stood in small groups, talking and laughing. One long table held a huge silver tea set, china cups and saucers, and platters of dainty cookies.

Elaine O'Brien hurried over. "I'm in charge of greeting prospective members, since I'm the honorable counselor of the Crystals." She beamed at Jill. "Come in and I'll introduce you around."

Elaine led Jill and Wendy to the center of the room and clapped her hands. "Attention, everyone! Attention, please." The girls stopped talking and turned to stare at the newcomers. "Allow me to introduce you to Jill Winters. She's the daughter of the famous Drew Winters and she's staying right here in our own town.

She wants to join the Crystals." Elaine waited while everyone clapped. Then she continued. "I'm hoping Jill will bring her father to one of our events later this summer."

Now the entire room broke into wild applause and excited whispers.

Jill stood stiff and uneasy under the girls' scrutiny. She wished she had stayed home.

Elaine stepped back as if seeing Wendy for the first time. "Oh, and this is Wendy Taylor, who also would like to join the Crystals. Wendy is staying with her aunt, Adrie Dekker, who owns the Tearoom Inn."

For a moment there was silence — and then a smattering of applause.

The Crystals quickly surrounded Jill, bombarding her with comments and questions.

"How wonderful that you're staying in our town!"

"How come you're not on tour with your dad?"

"I have all your father's records. Could you get him to autograph them?"

"Could your dad do a benefit for us? We'd make scads of money if he'd do it."

"I love how he sings 'Rhapsody.' It's my favorite song."

Wendy stood off to the side. This was not turning out well. She was being completely left out. Jill pushed through the group and stood close to Wendy, trying to include her friend in the conversations.

Jill was relieved when tea and cookies were served. She and Wendy sat together at a table with Elaine, Betty, and Gloria. Jill remembered how Quarry had spoken of them as "the big three."

"So how do you like the Crystals so far?" Gloria asked.

"Everyone seems friendly. What is the purpose of your club, anyway?" Jill asked. "I mean, I didn't hear anything about what you *do*."

"We do all sorts of things. We raise money and bake cookies for the servicemen," Betty answered. "We have war bond drives."

"Not to mention *lots of fun*! We'll have a big float in the parade on Saturday. We'll be having our formal dance, the Crystal Ball, soon. Don't you get the local paper?" Elaine asked. "There's always something about our activities in the paper."

"Then I guess it was the Crystals who sent flowers to Wendy and me when we arrived in Winter Haven," Jill said.

The three Crystals exchanged blank looks. "Er . . . oh, it probably *was* our group," Elaine said after an awkward pause. "We have a benevolence committee . . . it must have been them."

"A benevolence committee?" Jill asked.

"They're so busy doing good things for the community, it's hard to keep track sometimes," Betty answered. She made a sweeping gesture around the hall. "We get to use this hall because Reverend Bailey feels we're such good Christians."

Jill noticed a table in the corner of the hall with a box on it. On either side were dishes of white and black marbles. *The voting box.* She had a sick feeling in her stomach.

"Where is the powder room?" Wendy asked, getting up.

"Go out to the hall and turn right," Gloria told her.

When Wendy left, Elaine leaned over the table and spoke to Jill in a low voice. "Are you close friends with Wendy?"

"I met her on the train coming up here," Jill said. "And we've done a few things together. Why?"

"Well, we . . . we thought it was rather odd that you . . . ," Betty began.

"You're just not the same type . . . if you know what I mean . . . considering her background and all," Elaine said in a condescending tone.

Gloria looked uncomfortable. "Jill is new around here. So's her grandmother. They don't know . . ."

"Then we should tell her," Betty interrupted. "She should know who she's associating with. I'd want to know if I were Jill."

"Tell me what?"

"Don't repeat gossip," Gloria cautioned her friends.

"It's not gossip if it's *true*," Betty snapped. "And everyone knows it's true."

What were they talking about?

"I'll bet Wendy doesn't even know," Gloria said, "so we should be careful what we say."

"I don't want to hurt Wendy," Elaine said. "I know it's not Wendy's fault. Her mother is the one to blame."

"That's exactly what my mom said," Betty agreed. "She said, 'Be polite to Wendy. You don't have to associate with her, but you can be kind. It's not her fault that her mother . . .'"

Elaine put her hand up in a warning gesture. Wendy was heading back to the table. "We'll talk later," she whispered to Jill.

"I'm not sure I want to know." Jill stood up. "I'm going to the powder room."

Elaine got up too. "I'll come with you."

Once inside the bathroom, Elaine put her hand on Jill's arm. "You really don't know what we're talking about, do you?"

"No, I don't. If it's something bad about Wendy, I don't want to hear it." *Hear no evil.*

"It's not bad about Wendy really. As we said, it's not her fault." Elaine put her face close to Jill's and whispered. "Wendy is *illegitimate.* Her mother and father aren't married."

"What? Of course they're married," Jill retorted.

"Her parents are *not* married. No one knows who her father is."

Jill was lost. "What are you talking about?"

"Oh, Jill. I'm surprised you didn't figure it out yourself." Elaine rolled her eyes. "Adrie Dekker is Wendy's mother!"

17

Dark Secrets

Jill couldn't speak. Adrie, Wendy's mother? That couldn't be. This was just another one of the rumors spreading around town. "I don't believe a word you're saying."

"Jill, you must have seen the resemblance. Wendy's the spitting image of Adrie."

Of course Jill had seen the strong resemblance — the corn-silk blond hair and that single dimple. Could Elaine be telling the truth?

"I don't think Wendy knows this," Jill murmured.

"She may suspect," Elaine said, "but it's been

a secret for years—ever since Wendy was born. Adrie's sister brought Wendy up as her own daughter."

"How can you call it a secret if everyone knows but Wendy?"

"It's all Adrie's fault," Elaine said. "She got in a family way and disgraced herself. My mother told me all about it. Adrie went to Europe years ago and when she came back she was fat as a pig! She said she had put on weight from eating so much while she was away." Elaine waved her hand and snickered. "As if she could fool the whole town! Then she went off to *visit* her sister in New York. When she came back she was skinny as a snake. The easiest way out was to have the baby in New York and give it to her sister, who has no children. So Wendy's aunt Adrie is really her mother and her mother is really her aunt. You can understand why the Crystals probably won't invite Wendy into the club. She just doesn't fit under these circumstances . . . her mother being a tramp and all."

"Adrie Dekker isn't a tramp," Jill said, still trying to sort out all she was hearing.

"I can't believe a big-city girl from Boston could be so naive," Elaine said. "Adrie has men come to the inn a lot. Makes you wonder, doesn't it? And Wendy's just like her mother. She's a flirt too."

At that moment, Betty peeked into the powder room. "It's getting late and we have to clean up and vote. Are you two coming?"

Jill walked back into the hall as if in a trance. Wendy was waiting for her by the front door.

"Good-bye, Jill!" Betty called. "You'll be hearing from us."

The rest of the Crystals waved, "Bye, Jill! Bye, Wendy."

Before the door closed behind them, Jill could see Elaine placing the voting box on a table in the center of the hall.

Once they were outside, Wendy turned on Jill. "You spoiled everything!" Her face was drawn and white. "How *could* you?"

"How could I *what*? What are you talking about?"

"You set yourself up as the center of attention. You were so pushy! '*Drew Winters's daughter.*'

That's all I heard. I might as well have stayed home. No one paid one bit of attention to me."

Jill's own anger flared up. "I only came to this stupid meeting because you begged me to. *You're* the one who wanted to join, don't forget! I don't give one hoot about belonging to the Crystals— and you know that!"

"And just what took you so long in the powder room with Elaine? Talking about me?"

"I never said one bad thing about you!"

"Well, I'll soon find out. If I'm not invited to join the Crystals, it will be all your fault!" Wendy stormed off, leaving Jill standing alone on the sidewalk.

Jill needed to ring Nana but she didn't want to go back into the church to use the telephone. She never wanted to see the Crystals again. *Never!* The drugstore was closed. She spotted a phone booth outside the library, but when she got there, she discovered she didn't have a nickel to place the call.

She'd walk home. It was only a couple of miles. She crossed the street and started up the sidewalk by the docks. Even the cool sea air didn't clear her mind of the cobwebs that had been woven there by Elaine.

Adrie was Wendy's mother. Everyone in town seemed to know. And it was as if Wendy were some kind of criminal because of the circumstances of her birth. Jill walked faster as she recalled Wendy's outburst. How could Wendy say all those awful things? Jill kicked at a stone and tears welled up in her eyes. Elaine as much as said Wendy would be blackballed. And if Wendy was blackballed, she'd blame Jill!

Jill was unaware of the deepening darkness as she turned up the dirt road leading to Nana's house. Should she ring Wendy when she got home? No. Wendy should be the one to call and apologize. Nana would know what to do. She could hardly wait to get home.

She passed the trail that led off through the woods to Frenchman's Cove. The pathway was surrounded by overhanging trees and looked like a black tunnel.

Wait! What was that? A tiny light flickered deep in the woods—just a flicker. Someone was down there with a flashlight. Jill stopped, watching the blinking light as it came closer. Who would be down in Frenchman's Cove in the dark?

Jill tiptoed to a small grove of pine trees on the other side of the road and crouched behind the largest tree, hoping whoever it was would not cast the light in her direction. Footsteps crunched on the gravel as the flickering light came closer.

The light disappeared as the person turned onto another path—the one that led to Clayton Bishop's backyard. Jill peered out from her hiding place and cautiously started up the road again, removing her shoes to silence her steps. A light went on in the bungalow ahead. It must have been Clayton!

Jill stayed close to the other side of the road, trying to remain in the shadows as she passed by his cottage. Then, once around the bend, she flew toward the welcome sight of Nana's house.

Jill raced up the driveway, across the porch, and burst into the kitchen, slamming the door behind her.

"Jill! How did you get home?" Nana stopped putting away the supper dishes and stared at Jill's stocking feet. "Why didn't you ring?"

"I had to walk because . . ." She sank into a chair at the kitchen table and told Nana everything that happened at the Crystal's tea. "Nana, is it true what Elaine said about Adrie? Can she really be Wendy's mother?"

Nana sat down and traced the grain of the wood table with her finger. Finally she spoke. "I did once hear about Adrie being Wendy's mother after I first moved up here. You can't keep a secret like that in a small town. But it was never important to me. It's Adrie's business—not the town's business. Adrie made a mistake once in her life. Too bad the people here won't forget it. And it's too bad that stigma has to affect Wendy."

"Does Wendy know?"

"I honestly don't think so, although she may suspect, since they look so much alike." Nana seemed worried. "Were the girls mean to Wendy?"

"Yes. They weren't friendly at all to her and Wendy blamed *me*! She said if she's not accepted into the Crystals it'll be my fault. She was furious because the girls were gaga over Dad." Jill sat up in her chair angrily. "Wendy knew that the

Crystals would want me because of Daddy—and they'd only want her because she was my friend." Jill's voice rose. "So why is she mad at me?"

Nana shook her head. "Those girls believe Wendy's illegitimate and therefore they're too good for her. And I wouldn't be surprised if they're jealous because she's pretty and has nice clothes. Wendy, on the other hand, must feel left out in this town and she was hoping that being your friend would give *her* acceptance. When she didn't get the attention she craved by the Crystals, she blamed you." Nana got up to put the kettle on. "You know, Jill, she may call you tomorrow, to apologize."

"I'll feel uncomfortable with her now, since I learned Adrie is her mother and Wendy doesn't even know it." Jill took teacups from the cupboard. "Wendy did say she wished her aunt was her mother!"

"Jill, don't concern yourself with it. Try to forget about Wendy's problems."

While they sipped tea, Jill told Nana about Clayton Bishop coming out of the woods.

"Jill, you really shouldn't have come home

alone in the dark. Not that anything is likely to happen here, but . . . if I had known, I would have been worried."

"Well, I'm safe. Don't you worry, Nana." Jill was about to head for bed when the telephone rang. "Maybe it's Mom!" she yelled, running for the phone in the parlor.

It was Quarry. "I called to tell you that we may be on to somethin' after all—you know—about the strange goings-on." He lowered his voice. "I overheard Pa talkin' with the coast guard skipper."

"What did he say?"

"They think German U-boats are lyin' in wait somewhere round here. They stalk our ships and then blow 'em up."

"Quarry, my mom is coming back soon—across the Gulf." Jill reminded him. "She called last night."

"I don't mean to scare you. I'm just tellin' you what I heard, 'cause of the pigeon and all."

For a moment they were both silent. Then Quarry said, "Maybe we should tell someone about the bird and the message."

"Quarry," Jill whispered, shielding the telephone with her hand, "Nana and Ida Wilmar share some kind of secret. I heard them talking about it. I had put all that out of my mind, but now you tell me this. Someone around here may be helping the Germans. Ida is German. But Nana . . . she just *can't* be involved. We can't tell anyone yet. Not until we know more."

"Let's set the pigeon free tomorrow and see where it goes," Quarry suggested. "Then we'll decide what to do next."

Before Jill went to bed, she went up to the widow's walk. The sky was bright with stars and the waning full moon was setting over the church steeple. She could make out the constellation of Lyra overhead. Its brightest star, Vega, twinkled in the black sky. Daddy had shown her how to find Vega one night. "Make a wish," he had said.

The lights in the town were twinkling off. She could see the Tearoom Inn and thought about Adrie's secret. She wondered how many other secrets hovered over the town.

Jill folded her arms against the cold breeze and turned to the east. Out there in the black waters, U-boats were watching and waiting—like wolf packs, silently crouching, ready to spring.

Jill was about to descend the stairs but turned once more to survey the sea. It was difficult to see where the ocean met the sky until a sudden burst of light flashed on the horizon. The light dimmed, then disappeared.

Jill crawled down the stairs into the house, locking the door to the widow's walk behind her. In her room she pulled the window blinds, climbed into bed, and drew her down comforter around her. But she could not get warm.

She fingered the three wise monkeys on her bracelet. "Please, dear God, bring my mother and father home safely," she repeated over and over until she fell asleep.

18

The Pigeon Flies Home

All day Wednesday, Jill hoped that Wendy might ring and things would be all right between them. She was tempted to buzz Wendy herself, but when she remembered Wendy's accusations, she decided against it.

The telephone only rang once, and it was Quarry saying he was aback in his chores and had to work all day. He wouldn't be over until Thursday. Maybe they would let the pigeon go then.

Jill finally wrote a note to Dad, telling him how much she loved the bracelet and never took it off. "I don't worry half as much since I got my bracelet!" Jill wrote. She felt good after writing—it was as if she were talking with her father. She mailed it to his agent in Los Angeles because she wasn't sure where he was at this point. Was he flying to Las Vegas? San Diego? And then to New York? It was hard to keep up with his schedule. She prayed he would be safe, wherever he was.

After breakfast on Thursday, Jill was surprised to see three bicycles coming up the driveway.

"Oh, no! It's the big three! Nana, tell them I'm not here! Tell them I'm sick or something!"

"I can't do that, Jill," Nana said.

"I don't want them to stay. What'll I do?"

"Go outside and see what they want. You don't have to invite them in."

Jill went out to the porch. "Hi," she said. "What brings you here?"

"We wanted to deliver the good news to you ourselves, instead of mailing a letter," Elaine said, handing Jill a white envelope.

"Open it," Betty said. "It's your invitation to join the Crystals! You were voted into the club unanimously."

Gloria was beaming. "Congratulations, Jill. We're really glad that you're going to be one of us."

Jill took the envelope but didn't open it. "What about Wendy?"

Betty shook her head. "She didn't make it, Jill. She isn't right for our group."

Elaine moved closer to Jill and spoke in a low, confidential tone. "You understand, don't you? I explained why she couldn't be one of the Crystals—with her background and everything."

"Just between us, Jill, every single blackball was used," Betty said. "It's the first time that ever happened. We've had a few blackballs used in the past—and of course even one would keep the person out—but Wendy, poor thing, was not acceptable. She's just not the right material for the Crystals."

Jill had a sick feeling in the pit of her stomach. "Did you tell her yet?"

"We stopped by her house and slipped the envelope under the door. We didn't knock. It would be embarrassing for her to face us," Elaine said. "It's better this way."

Betty nodded her agreement.

"We sent a nice note," Gloria hastened to say.

"How thoughtful of you," Jill said, her anger mounting.

"So . . . don't you just love living here at your grandmother's? It's a beautiful old house." Betty waited, as if expecting to be invited in.

Jill said nothing and after an awkward moment, Elaine asked, "Is your father coming up here this summer?"

"I don't know," Jill answered coldly.

"We'd just *love* to meet him in person," Betty said.

"When he comes, I'm sure he'd like to be left alone," Jill said, turning toward the kitchen door.

"The next meeting of the Crystals will be in two weeks. But we'll see you before then, won't we?" Gloria asked. "Maybe at the clambake on Saturday?"

"Would you like to ride on our float in the parade?" Betty asked. "We'd be right honored to have Drew Winters's daughter on board." She turned to the others. "Wouldn't we?"

"Oh yes, Jill. Do join us," Elaine pleaded.

"We'll be startin' the parade at Town Hall. Just come down on Saturday morning. Wear something patriotic. We're a very patriotic group."

"No, I can't ride on the float," Jill replied quickly. "I've got to go now. My grandmother wants me. We're . . . busy."

"Oh . . . well, good-bye," Elaine looked bewildered.

"Good-bye," Jill managed to say before shutting the door behind her. She peeked out the window and watched the three girls leave on their bicycles. "I hate them! They're horrible!"

"What happened?" Nana asked. "Weren't you invited to join?"

"Oh, sure I was. After all, I'm Drew Winters's daughter." Jill threw the invitation on the table. "They even want me to ride on their stupid float in the parade."

"What's wrong, Jill?"

"They blackballed Wendy! Just like I knew they would!" Jill paced the kitchen, angrily. "They didn't even have the decency to face her. They put a letter under her door."

"How very mean!"

Jill sank into a chair. "Wendy's going to blame me." Tears surged up in her eyes.

"Do you want to ring her?" Nana asked.

"And have her scream at me? No."

"Do you want me to talk to her aunt, er . . . mother?"

"I don't know. Adrie seemed to know this was going to happen. She warned us."

"What did you tell the girls from the Crystals?"

"I didn't say one word. I was too flustered. I should have thrown their invitation back in their faces."

"Oh, don't bring trouble on yourself. They're not worth it. Just don't bother going to their meetings. They'll get the message." Nana shook her head. "I do feel badly for Wendy, though."

Jill went out to the porch and sat by the window. Had Wendy seen the envelope from the Crystals yet? Jill had promised to be a good friend, no matter what. And now Wendy thought Jill had betrayed her.

A radio news program interrupted her thoughts. "Another merchant ship was torpedoed in the North Atlantic last night." The rest was muffled as Nana quickly turned down the volume.

Jill leaned back on the cushions of the window seat and closed her eyes. *See no evil; hear no evil.* But it was too late.

Quarry arrived with his lunch after noon, and he and Jill ate outside on the picnic bench. Later, when Nana went down to the point to finish up her painting of the lighthouse, Jill said, "Let's take the pigeon to the widow's walk and release it now."

"What about the message?"

"I'll put it back on the bird's leg. That way no one'll know that it was intercepted." Jill went up to her room to retrieve the capsule from a sock in her bureau drawer.

While Quarry held the pigeon fast, Jill replaced the band on its leg. She gently set the bird in a covered picnic basket she found in the pantry, then they climbed up to the widow's walk.

It was warm on the lookout, with only a slight breeze dappling the sea. "It's a good day to fly," Quarry said, adjusting a pair of binoculars. "I told my pa we were bird-watchin'."

They each looped the straps of their binoculars around their necks. Jill brought the basket to the railing. "Here we go," she said, opening the cover.

The bird was huddled in the basket. Quarry held the container while Jill gathered the bird into her hands. "Fly home!" She tossed the pigeon into the air. It flapped its wings uncertainly, then landed on the railing. "Shoo!" Jill waved at the bird. It fluttered to another spot on the balustrade. "It doesn't want to fly!"

"It's gettin' its bearings," Quarry assured her. "Just wait."

The bird hopped hesitantly on the rail, then suddenly soared into the air. "There it goes!" Jill cried.

The bird flew around the widow's walk a few times, then began to fly in wider and wider circles. After a few moments it turned and headed northwest. Jill and Quarry watched through the binoculars as the pigeon flew directly to Clayton Bishop's pigeon coop.

19

Bad News from Europe

"I knew it!" Jill whooped. "Clayton's birds are carrier pigeons!"

"He did sell squab to Adrie's inn, though."

"That must be just a cover-up," Jill insisted.

"Okay, now that we know, shouldn't we tell my pa or the sheriff or someone?"

"We need more proof that he's really helping the Germans."

"What more proof do you want, Jill?"

"Quarry, we need to know who *sent* the bird. The bird and the message were sent to Clayton by *someone else*, right? That's who we've got to locate now."

"Okay, Jill." Quarry put up his hands in surrender. "And just how do we do that?"

"I don't know. We've got to be cautious about asking questions or telling anyone. Besides, Clayton might wonder why the bird was so late. He might suspect it's been intercepted."

"Let's get down from here," Quarry said nervously. "Clayton could be lookin' up here right now and connectin' the bird to us."

"You're right. You fold the chairs and lay them flat so they can't be seen. We've got to be *real* careful from now on." As Jill picked up the picnic basket she remembered something. "Quarry, I saw Clayton Bishop heading to that path in the woods carrying a covered basket. I'll bet he's taking a bird to someone. That way, when the other person needs to send a message, he simply lets the bird fly it back to Clayton."

"There's no one for miles around out there at Frenchman's Cove."

"He's taking something out there. I'm certain of that."

Once they were on the sunporch, Jill told Quarry about the Crystals blackballing Wendy.

"I kinda thought that might happen. I told you they're a bunch o' snobs."

"Is there any reason Wendy might be barred— other than the fact she's a summercater?" Jill watched his face carefully, wondering what he knew about Wendy's family.

"Well . . . there's been rumors. I don't want to repeat them."

"About Wendy?" Jill waited. Then she added, "And about Adrie?"

"Well . . . yeah. I guess you know, then," Quarry said, "about Adrie bein' Wendy's mom."

"Has Wendy heard this?"

"I don't think so. She hasn't been up here very much—I think last summer was the first time she ever came without her folks and she was only here for a couple o' weeks."

"Just long enough to be snubbed," Jill said. At that moment the telephone rang and Jill ran to answer it.

"Please let me speak to Elizabeth." Ida Wilmar sounded upset. "I need her right away."

"Are you all right, Mrs. Wilmar?"

"No, something terrible has happened. I must speak to Elizabeth at once."

"She's out on the point, but I'll go get her."

"No . . . tell her please to come over here quickly. *Danke* . . . Thank you." She hung up.

Jill raced out the back door and headed for the point. "Nana! Come quickly!"

"What's wrong?" Her grandmother stood up.

"Ida needs you right away!" Jill panted as she met her grandmother on the lawn. "She said something terrible has happened. But she didn't say what! You better go now."

Nana hurried to the car and drove down the driveway.

"Can I help?" Quarry asked.

"Let's pick up Nana's paints and things," Jill said.

After Quarry went home, Jill paced the floor, looking out the window every few moments. Several times she was tempted to ring Mrs. Wilmar's house, then changed her mind. Nana knew she was worried and she'd call when she could.

When the phone finally rang, Jill grabbed it.

"Ida is coming home with me to spend the night. Would you throw something together for supper, honey? Anything will be fine. Maybe an omelet?"

Jill pared potatoes and put them on to boil. She grated hard cheese from the cupboard and got out the eggs. She was setting the table when Nana pulled into the driveway.

Nana and Ida came into the kitchen. They both looked grim and Jill didn't dare to ask any questions.

Nana glanced at the table and smiled at Jill. "Everything looks nice, dear. Thank you."

"I'll put the eggs on now," said Jill. "Supper will be ready soon." She could hear their voices as they went upstairs.

Jill drained the potatoes and tossed in some oleomargarine. Then she poured beaten eggs into a sizzling pan and added the cheese. Mom had tried to teach her to make omelets by turning the pan gently and sliding a knife along the edges. Jill never could get the hang of it. The omelet would break and they'd both end up laughing. As she was thinking about it, this omelet broke too. Oh, never mind, Jill thought, scrambling it all together. She was putting the food onto the plates when Nana and Ida came downstairs.

Before eating, Nana held Ida's and Jill's hands and offered the blessing. "Thank you, Lord, for this food and for our families. Please guard our loved ones wherever they are." Jill could see a tear slip down Ida's cheek and again she wondered what had happened that was so terrible. But they didn't talk about it.

After dinner they all went out to the sunporch. A cold breeze drifted through the open windows, so Nana shut them. Outside the stars were bright and the lighthouse across the channel sent its long rays over the water. Nana closed the darkening blinds, then turned on a table lamp. After helping Ida into a chaise longue, she covered her with an afghan. "You sit there and relax, dear," she said gently. "Things will seem brighter in the morning."

Nana sat down next to Jill on the window seat. "Jill, Ida received a letter from Switzerland today. It took almost a month to get here. Her cousin managed to escape from Germany a few months ago and wrote to say that Ida's husband was arrested last year and taken away to some kind of prison camp."

"Oscar, my husband, he is Jewish," Ida explained. "That madman, Adolf Hitler, is terrorizing Jews in Germany, taking their businesses and separating families, and Gott knows vat else."

"Why?" Jill asked.

"Hitler is evil. He breeds hate and cruelty and everything that's wicked." Ida's voice was full of contempt. "Ve're hearing more and more about the terrible things he's doing to the Jews—and to other groups of innocent people, too."

"Do you know where Mr. Wilmar is or how he is?"

"*Nein.* My cousin says that people taken to such camps disappear forever." She pulled a folded handkerchief from the sleeve of her sweater. "I vill never see my Oscar again. I know that now." She wiped her eyes.

Jill's eyes filled with tears and she jumped up to throw her arms around Ida. "I wish I could help you," she whispered. "I hate this war."

"You are a sweet child," Ida murmured. "I tell you vhat. Vill you call me *Tante Ida*? May I be your aunt? I have no family anymore."

"Yes, you can be my aunt, Tante Ida," Jill said, struggling not to cry. How could anyone in this town suspect Ida of sympathizing with the Nazis? How could Jill herself have ever thought anything so stupid?

20

The Ring

On Friday, Tante Ida and Nana combined some of their ration stamps, bought groceries, and spent the morning cooking. Jill helped to make *Sonnenblumenbrot*, a German sunflower bread, and *Apfelkuchen*, an apple cake. Tante Ida seemed to be feeling more relaxed.

Jill took a deep breath and asked, "Tante Ida, can you tell me what the word *sonnabend* means? Is it a German word?"

"*Ja*, it's German. *Sonnabend* means 'Saturday,'" Ida answered.

But that's not what Quarry had said. "Is there another word for Saturday?"

"*Ja, Samstag.* But *sonnabend* means 'Saturday night'—going towards Sunday. Why do you ask?"

"Er . . . I heard you use the word when you were talking to Nana the other night."

"Oh, *ja,* that was vhen we were planning to get together on Saturday evening, instead of our usual Sunday evening." Tante Ida smiled. "I sometimes fall back into German vhen I speak."

So Nana and Ida really *were* planning to change their regular meeting to Saturday. That was all right, then. Jill still wondered about their secret, though. And the pigeon's message.

While they were eating lunch at the picnic table, a boy rode up on a bicycle with a yellow envelope. Nana stood up right away, her face suddenly pale.

"*Mein Gott!*" Ida whispered, thrusting her hand over her heart.

Telegrams usually meant someone had died.

"I have a telegram for Miss Jill Winters," the messenger announced.

"For Jill?" Nana asked.

"That's me," said Jill. She opened the envelope with shaking hands.

"What does it say?" Nana asked nervously, looking over Jill's shoulder.

"It's from Mom!" Jill read it out loud:

HAVE NON-PRIORITY RESERVATIONS ON CARIBOU TO NOVA SCOTIA. STOP. HOME NEXT WEEK. STOP. SEE YOU SOON. STOP. LOVE MOM.

Jill waved the telegram in the air and did a little dance. "Yippee! Mom's coming home next week!"

"Wonderful! What a relief!" Nana exclaimed.

"*Wunderbar!*" Tante Ida chimed in.

"Your dad may be finished with his tour around that time. I'll be so relieved when our whole family is together again, safe and sound," Nana said.

Later in the afternoon, Jill received a telephone call from Elaine. "Hi! Just wanted to remind you to get down to the town hall early tomorrow morning so you can ride on the float with us."

"I told you I can't make it," Jill said. "I have other plans."

There was long pause. Then Elaine said, "Well, if you change your mind, come down."

"Thank you," said Jill, hanging up.

Jill thought about Wendy again. She hadn't heard from her since they went to the Crystals' tea. Was she still mad? Would she be going to the clambake? Did she know that Quarry was going with Jill?

"I'm going to ride over to Wendy's," she told Nana. "I don't know if she'll even talk to me, but I've decided to face her anyway."

"Good luck, honey," Nana said.

Clayton's car was in the driveway as Jill rode by his house. She pedaled slowly but saw no sign of him.

Jill passed Guy Binette's store and stopped to see Quarry. "I'm going over to Wendy's, but I'm sure I won't be there long. Are you coming to my house this afternoon? We can ride together when I head back."

"I can't, Jill. I have to work all day today. Guy is stocking up on things for the holiday weekend."

"Ida Wilmar spent the night with us. Quarry, it's so sad. She just heard that her husband was arrested by the Nazis. She doesn't think she'll ever see him again." Jill paused. "She's certainly not a Nazi sympathizer."

"Don't rule her out yet," Quarry said. "Not until we know who sent the bird. You said that yourself."

"I know, but I'm pretty sure it's not her. I asked Tante Ida what *sonnabend* means and she told me. It means Saturday evening. She came right out and told me."

"*Tante* Ida?"

"She asked me if she could be my aunt."

Jill was about to leave when Quarry said, "I'll come over to your house about noontime tomorrow and we can ride to the clambake together."

"Okay, Quarry."

Jill rode up the sidewalk to the Tearoom Inn, parked her bike, then hesitated. Did she really want to see Wendy? After all, Wendy was the one who should be apologizing. Still, it was a pretty mean thing the Crystals had done and Jill needed Wendy to know she had no part in it.

She walked up the steps and although the door to the lobby was open, Jill rang the bell and waited.

Adrie came to the door. Her eyes narrowed when she saw Jill. "Just what do *you* want?"

Jill bit her lip. "I was hoping to see Wendy."

"Well, she doesn't want to see *you!*" Adrie towered in the doorway. Jill recalled Quarry's description of her. *Icebound.*

"I feel terrible about what the Crystals did. I—I want Wendy to know that," Jill stammered.

"You're responsible for all this, Jill. You're the one who caused all this trouble for Wendy." Adrie turned and disappeared into the other room as Wendy approached the open door.

"What is it, Jill?" Wendy said in a flat tone.

"I haven't heard from you and I . . ." Jill waited, but Wendy said nothing. "I . . . felt really awful after you walked away on Tuesday night, and I was hoping . . ."

"Hoping what? That we'd still be friends?"

"Yes," Jill answered. "I'm not joining the Crystals, Wendy. I think they're rude and cruel. I never wanted to join in the first place. You wanted me to try to get us both in. Remember?"

"I remember." Wendy's mouth was a tight line. "And I remember that Quarry was a good friend of mine too, before you came along. I know he invited you to the clambake."

"How did you find out about that?"

"It doesn't matter where I heard it. What did you tell Quarry about me?"

"Nothing! Wendy, you and I and Quarry are good friends. Remember my promise? I promised to be a good friend no matter what and I meant it." Jill fought back tears and swallowed hard to keep her voice from breaking. "I just wanted to tell you that I still am your friend. If you want me to be, that is."

Wendy's eyes flashed with icy anger. "I don't care whether you or Quarry want to be my friends, Jill." She shrugged. "I told Aunt Adrie all about you and the Crystals and what happened on Tuesday. We had a long talk. You know what? Aunt Adrie and I don't need you or anyone else in this town. We're just fine, my aunt and I. In fact, I've never felt better."

It was as if Wendy were someone else altogether. The change was total. *Icebound.*

"Well, if you change your mind, give me a buzz," Jill said. She waited for a response, but none came.

Wendy shut the door with a click, but not before Jill saw something shining on Wendy's finger. The pigeon-blood ruby ring!

If Wendy and Adrie had talked, then surely she must finally know Adrie's secret. That must be why Adrie had given her daughter her ruby ring.

Wendy had wished Adrie was her mother. Now her wish had come true. Maybe she felt she belonged to someone at last. Maybe she wouldn't need to make up fantastic stories to get attention. Anyway, Jill had done what she needed to do—to offer her friendship. If Wendy didn't need it or want it—well, there was nothing Jill could do about that.

As soon as Jill got home she told Nana and Ida about her visit to Wendy's.

"She seemed to have become like Adrie," Jill said. "You know . . . cold and . . . different. I don't think Wendy will ever be my friend again."

"*Ende* . . . endings," said Tante Ida sadly. "Life is full of endings. We have to accept this."

Jill went to her room and flung herself onto the bed. The wind whistled around the windows. The waves crashed against the rocks.

Endings were hard to accept.

21

The Clambake

Saturday, July fourth, was clear and calm. "Are you going to the parade, Jill?" Nana asked.

"No," Jill answered. The very thought of seeing the Crystals waving and throwing kisses from their float made her feel ill. She knew the Crystals would be at the clambake, but at least there'd be lots of other people there too. She decided she would stick close to Quarry.

She put on her new white clam diggers, halter top, and shoes. She brushed her hair and tied it with a red ribbon she found in Nana's sewing box. Then she applied three coats of Tangee on her lips. If Nana noticed, she didn't object. "You look so chic!" she said.

Tante Ida agreed. *"Du bist wie eine Blume.* You are as lovely as a flower."

Nana pulled Jill's navy blue sweater from the hall closet. "Take this along, honey. You'll be glad to have it. It can get cold on the beach, especially toward evening." She held up the sweater. "This is such a beautiful sweater with that cute sailor collar. Did your mother make it?"

"Yes, she stayed up all night one night to finish it," Jill said.

"Your mother loves you a lot." Nana handed Jill the sweater. "Oh, I meant to tell you that we won't be here when you get home. We'll be at Ida's, and I probably won't get back until eleven or later." Nana pointed to the kitchen door. "I always leave a key out there under the doormat, Jill."

"Okay." Jill kissed her grandmother good-bye. "Bye, Nana. Bye, Tante Ida." She ran outside.

"Wow, you look swell, all decked out," Quarry said with a shy grin. He wore freshly pressed brown knee-length shorts and a tan shirt. His auburn hair was neatly combed, but wayward strands flipped into his eyes.

He is quite handsome, Jill thought, blushing as she tucked her sweater into the bicycle basket.

Quarry pushed off on his bicycle. "Let's go!" Jill followed him down the dirt road. They both slowed as they passed Clayton Bishop's. There were no signs of anyone, although his car was parked in the driveway.

They headed through the town, where red, white, and blue streamers decorated every lamppost and building. The streets were littered with paper candy wrappers and other clutter from the morning's parade.

They took the road that led to the lighthouse, then turned off onto the dirt road to the beach. Cars were parked on both sides and people were carrying folding chairs and blankets down to the sand. In the distance, Jill could see streams of smoke.

"They've already dug the pits and got the fires going," Quarry explained. "Let's leave our bikes here." He pointed to a stand of pine trees where other bikes were stacked.

Jill grabbed her sweater and Quarry took a plaid blanket from his bicycle basket.

When they got close to the water, Quarry spread out the blanket on the sand. Jill found rocks and shells to hold down the corners. They put their shoes on the blanket and walked toward the smoky haze where the wood fires had burned. Men in white aprons were raking the hot ashes.

"These pits are filled with wood and flat rocks," Quarry explained. "They lit the fires early this morning, so the rocks could get white-hot. They must be ready 'cause they're fillin' the pits now."

A truck full of green vegetation pulled up to the smoking trenches. "What are they doing?" Jill asked. "That looks like seaweed!"

"It *is*! They toss seaweed on top of each layer of food."

The fires hissed and a salty smell filled the air as the smoke billowed. Jill and Quarry watched while chicken, buckets of clams, green lobsters, and unhusked corn were layered into the smoldering pits. After a final mound of seaweed was added, the trenches were covered with canvas to keep the steam in.

"Everything will smell and taste of the sea," Quarry told her. "Let's take a walk while it's cookin'."

Jill and Quarry meandered along the beach where picnic tables had been set up. Some were makeshift plywood balanced on sawhorses. There were piles of newspapers, paper plates, and stacks of paper towels on each table, held down by rocks or shells.

"A real clambake ain't got linen tablecloths, ya know," Quarry said. He nudged Jill. "Even the Rocks and Crystals eat off newspapers at a clambake."

Elaine, Betty, and Gloria were sitting on a table, laughing and chatting with a group of boys. They hushed when they caught sight of Jill.

"Well, well," Elaine said. "If it isn't Jill Winters! So you've decided to honor us with your presence?" She turned to the boys. "This is Drew Winters's daughter. She was invited to join the Crystals, but evidently we're not good enough for *her*."

Gloria looked uncomfortable. "Don't be so mean, Elaine."

"We even asked her to ride in the float this

mornin'. But she never showed up," Betty added.

"Come on, Jill," Quarry said, taking her hand and leading her away.

"She's a real snob," Elaine whispered—loud enough for Jill to hear.

Jill wheeled around. "You Crystals are the snobs. You're mean and hateful—you and your vicious ballot box. I wouldn't be a Crystal for a million dollars."

"Oh, she's upset about *Wendy*," Elaine said to the others.

"Well, look who she came here with—Quarry! You know the old sayin': Birds of a feather flock together!" said one of the boys with a sneer.

The Rocks are as bad as the Crystals, Jill thought.

Quarry hustled Jill away. "Come on, Jill. They ain't worth it."

Jill was shaking. "They think they're such good citizens with their *benevolence committee!*" she sputtered as they stomped back to their blanket. "Why, they've probably destroyed Wendy's life—not to mention all the other girls they've blackballed!"

"I hope they didn't spoil the picnic for you," Quarry said as they sat down.

"No, siree! It felt good to tell them off. Someone should have done it a long time ago." She punched Quarry's arm lightly. "Let's have a great time today," she said. "When do we eat?"

Jill and Quarry had their plates piled high. Quarry showed Jill how to crack open her bright red lobster and how to lift the skin from the necks of the clams and dip the meat into melted butter.

"Everything is delicious," Jill said, biting into a steaming ear of corn. "I'm glad you invited me, Quarry."

Later, as the sun was beginning to set, a man played an accordion and another called dance steps though a megaphone. Several couples began to square-dance on the sand. "Come on," Quarry said, pulling Jill into a square.

"I don't know how!"

"We'll show you," the others said. "You'll catch on."

Soon Jill was swinging and promenading with Quarry and the rest of her square. Before long, she was able to change corners and keep up with the others.

"I've never had such fun!" she told Quarry breathlessly. "Not everyone from this town is a stuck-up snob like the Crystals. Too bad Wendy didn't come, though. She would have had a good time."

Suddenly the music stopped. "May I have your attention," the announcer said. "I hate to be the bearer of bad news."

Jill clutched Quarry's arm.

"I've just received tragic information. Paulie Binette, whom most of you have known all his life—Guy Binette's only son—has been killed in action in the Pacific." The man paused as the audience erupted with cries, then continued. "His father was informed this afternoon."

"Oh, no! Poor Mr. Binette," Jill murmured.

"Paulie was all Guy had left," said Quarry sadly.

"I hope our community can pitch in and help Guy get through this sad time," the announcer said.

Silence settled on the once-happy crowd.

Then a man yelled, "We should *not* be enjoyin' ourselves, when our boys are being killed in this damned war!"

"No more clambakes or parades for the duration," someone else cried out.

"Let's go, Jill," Quarry said. "I think I should be with Guy—or at least offer to help."

"We'll ride to town together and then I'll go on home by myself, Quarry. Don't worry about me."

"I brought you here, Jill, and I should see you home," Quarry insisted.

"No, you've got to help Mr. Binette. It's more important. I'll be fine."

"Here, Jill, take my flashlight. It might be dark by the time you get to your road." Quarry placed the flashlight in her bicycle basket. "I'll ring you when I get back home."

Jill and Quarry rode silently to town.

After Quarry left, Jill pedaled toward the harbor road. Mr. Binette would be replacing the blue star with a gold one on the flag in his shop-window, signifying that the serviceman in his house had been killed. Paulie had died in the

Pacific front, which meant he was killed by the Japanese, not the Germans. That was on the other side of the world. Was there anyplace on earth that wasn't fighting? Even here in Winter Haven people like the Crystals were cruel and full of hate. Jill turned onto Harbor Road and stopped to pull a tissue from her pocket, when suddenly she saw a car rounding the corner from Main Street.

Could it be Nana? No, it was too early. It must be someone going to Clayton Bishop's house. Quickly Jill hopped on her bicycle and steered into the cluster of pines where she had hidden before.

The car barreled up the road, turned into Clayton's driveway, then made its way between the house and the garage and into the backyard. Adrie's car! Jill stayed in the pine trees and watched as Adrie went into the house. What was going on?

22

Monster from the Sea

Jill watched and waited from her secluded spot among the trees. She pulled her sweater from the bike basket and tied it around her waist. It was big and dark enough to cover most of her white pants.

Adrie and Clayton suddenly came out of the house and went into the backyard.

Were they going for a drive? There was no sound of an engine starting. What were they doing? They seemed to have disappeared.

Jill pedaled to the overgrown path she had passed so many times. She could see nothing through the dark tunnel of trees but she was certain that Adrie and Clayton were ahead of her on this pathway leading to Frenchman's Cove.

Jill hesitated. Should she follow them? Should she ride home and ring for the police? What could she tell them? She had no proof of anything. And she no longer had the pigeon and its suspicious German message as evidence.

Quarry had said German submarines were torpedoing many ships on the East Coast. Could there be a submarine hiding somewhere nearby? No, that was totally unreasonable. The U.S. Navy had a radio interception station a short way up the road. They were supposed to know if submarines were in this area, weren't they? She turned to head home, then stopped.

Suppose that Adrie and Clayton really *were* involved in helping the Germans. Wasn't it her patriotic duty to find out and report them? She should follow them. If she discovered something was wrong, then she'd sneak back and ring the sheriff.

Jill pedaled a little way down the pathway, but the muddy ground was rough. She'd have to follow them on foot. She hid the bicycle in the bushes, leaving Quarry's flashlight in the basket. Then she crept down the path into the darkening woods.

She passed the other trail—the one that led off to the right to Clayton's backyard. There was no one in sight. But straight ahead in the distance she could see the flicker of a flashlight and, cautiously, she followed. Her rope-soled shoes were quiet on the thick carpet of pine needles.

The path led deeper and deeper into the woods, twisting and winding, until Jill lost her sense of direction. Tree limbs snagged her hair and clothing. A hundred yards or more ahead, Clayton and Adrie seemed unaware of Jill's presence.

After a while, a freshening breeze carried the sound of ocean waves and the smell of the sea. Emerging from the woods, Jill found herself atop a cliff overlooking the water. In the dusk the shadowy figures in front of her were descending a steep path that snaked its way down to a desolate cove.

Jill did not dare get any closer. She crouched behind a cleft in the rocks. Clayton and Adrie were standing on the rocky beach, looking out to sea. They flashed their lights on and off. Were they signaling someone? Who? Jill couldn't see any boats nearby.

Suddenly the water in the cove became turbulent and the surface of the sea ripped apart. A dark shape arose from the depths. Breakers lifted and crested around it, as if some monstrous sea-creature had been aroused from sleep. A German submarine! On its side was a number: *U-1230*.

Waves heaved as the gigantic ship settled. Water cascaded from its turret. Within seconds, figures appeared on the deck of the U-boat and a rubber raft was dropped into the water. Jill strained her eyes against the deepening darkness. Three men rowed swiftly to the shore where Adrie and Clayton waited.

When the small boat reached the beach, Clayton pulled it onto the sand and two of the men climbed from the raft. The group spoke to each other for a few moments, then Clayton shoved the raft out and the third man paddled back toward the submarine, where he was hoisted onto the deck. There were no lights on the ship and the flashlights on the shore had been extinguished.

The U-boat lay silently on the surface of the fjord, like an apparition. This must have been one of the ships that had torpedoed so many vessels along the coast.

Jill wanted to see if the U-boat would submerge again, but then she realized with a start that Adrie, Clayton, and the other two men were halfway up the path, headed in her direction!

Jill had to get out of there! If she ran ahead of them, they would surely see her. She moved around to the other side of the boulder and flattened herself into a crevasse. She held her breath as their footsteps came closer. She could hear them whispering but she didn't understand their language.

What would they do if they found her? Jill realized that neither Adrie nor Clayton would show her any mercy. If she were caught, they'd probably dump her body into the ocean and no one would ever know what happened. If only she had gone home, instead of putting herself in such danger. She huddled perfectly still as the group passed on the other side of the boulder. At the top of the cliff, they turned down the path that led back to Harbor Road.

Jill waited until they had gone far ahead and turned on their flashlights. She could see where they were and paced herself accordingly.

It was pitch-black in the woods now. Although the air was cold, Jill's face was sweaty and her hair hung in limp strands. She brushed it back from her forehead, then gasped. Where was her ribbon? It had been tied to her hair when she left the clambake. Oh no! It must be snagged in a tree somewhere!

She paused to pull out a stick that was caught in her rope sole. When she looked up, she saw the group ahead of her flashing their lights on something. Her ribbon? She slipped behind a tree just as the men looked in her direction. Did they suspect someone had followed them? Did they see her?

After a moment, the lights ahead began to bob—they were walking again. The flickering lights turned left and disappeared. They were heading for Clayton's backyard.

As soon as Jill had safely passed the trail to Clayton's she raced to her bike, climbed on, and rode out of the woods—just as Adrie's car roared down the street toward her! The half-blacked-out headlights beamed directly on Jill. The car screeched to a stop and backed up.

Adrie shrieked, *"Kriege sie!"* to Clayton, who was standing in the driveway.

"Ich gehe schnell!" Clayton responded. Adrie then took off down the road toward town.

Jill heard a car door slam and an engine start-ing. She pedaled frantically up the road and around the bend. There was no place to hide. Nana's house was just a little farther. Could she make it? The house was still dark. Nana wasn't home yet. Jill pushed the pedals with all her might when, BANG! The front tire burst and the handlebars twisted in her hands, throwing Jill to the ground.

She untangled herself from the bicycle as Clayton's car came around the curve. Her arm was bleeding and her leg hurt. She grabbed Quarry's flashlight from the basket. If Clayton caught her, the heavy flashlight would be her weapon. She limped up the driveway as fast as she could, onto the porch, where she lifted the door-mat and found the key. Fumbling, she put it into the lock with shaking hands. The door burst open. Jill flew inside and bolted it behind her.

Clayton's car was idling in the driveway now. Jill raced up to the stairway that led to the widow's walk. She heard a window breaking somewhere in the house and scrambled up the flight of stairs. Her left leg throbbed as she tried to climb and hold on to the flashlight. Jill groped around the frame of the hatch door for the bolt. She heard footsteps on the hall stairs. She nearly dropped the flashlight, but finally her fingers circled the handle and she released the lock. Jill rammed her arms and shoulders against the heavy door until it lifted. Then she clambered onto the roof and silently lowered the trapdoor. After fastening a bolt, she huddled on the floor.

Please, God, don't let him find me, she prayed.

23

Trapped

Jill lay shaking on the floor of the widow's walk. Clayton Bishop was searching the house. She could hear him in the stairwell below and feel the vibrations as he came up the stairs. Clayton was just beneath the hatch door, banging and trying to push his way onto the roof. What would he do to Jill if he found her?

Oh, Nana, please come home!

Then another thought shot through her. No! Nana *mustn't* come home. Not with Clayton Bishop here!

She heard the telephone ringing. The banging stopped and Clayton descended the stairs. The phone continued ringing. Could it be Quarry? Maybe he'd be worried and come looking for her. Then he'd be in danger too! She had put so many people in jeopardy, just because she hadn't trusted anyone.

The telephone finally stopped ringing and the house was silent. Where was Clayton? She lay still, listening intently.

Suddenly a car started up in the driveway. Jill crept to the side of the railing and peeked over the rim. Clayton was leaving!

Jill waited until the car went around the bend and out of sight, then ran to the hatch door. She pulled at the bolt and tried to lift the door with both hands. It wouldn't open! She rattled it and pushed. But the door was sealed shut. Clayton had thrown the bolt on the other side and imprisoned Jill on the widow's walk. He'd locked her up to give himself time to get away!

Jill rattled the door and screamed, "Let me out! Help!"

Then she remembered Quarry's flashlight. She felt around the floor of the deck. There!

"Come on, Quarry. Look this way," she whispered as she began clicking the light in the direction of the lighthouse. Three dots, three dashes, three dots. SOS. That was the international distress code she'd learned in school.

She flashed the beam on and off until her fingers were sore. "Please look over here, Quarry, *please.*"

Dot, dot, dot. Dash, dash, dash. Dot, dot, dot.

House lights in the town were blinking off. Jill wished she had her binoculars. She could see the Tearoom Inn and make out the half-painted headlights of cars as they moved down Main Street. Was Adrie getting away with her German agents?

What a dimwit I was, Jill thought. It's so obvious now that Adrie's inn was a cover-up—a front for foreign agents! Who would question vacationers showing up at an inn?

Adrie was so clever! She knew that Jill had seen the pigeons the day she fell off her bicycle. That's why she'd taken off in such a hurry. Adrie must have gone directly to Clayton's house to figure out a way to throw Jill off track. Then, when

Nana went to the store that day she had seen Adrie's car in Clayton's backyard.

It was out of character for Adrie Dekker to suddenly invite Nana and Jill to a squab dinner. Adrie was not the neighborly type.

To think I fell for it! And all the time I was suspecting people I should have trusted—like Nana and Tante Ida.

Dot, dot, dot. Dash, dash, dash. Dot, dot, dot.

Jill flashed the light more urgently. "Please see the light, Quarry." But the flashlight gradually grew dim as the batteries gave out. It was cold and she was shivering. She untied the sweater from her waist and put it on.

How long had Jill been on the roof? Nana should have been home ages ago.

It seemed as if she'd been on the roof for hours, when Jill finally saw faint lights coming up the road. Four vehicles. One of them was Nana's car. Two others were police cars. She recognized Hugh MacDonald's truck. Quarry must have seen her signal! They all stopped in the driveway and got out of their vehicles.

"Help!" she screamed. "I'm trapped up here!"

"We're comin'!" Quarry yelled, looking up.

Moments later, Nana unbolted the trapdoor and Jill fell into her arms.

On the sunporch, Nana tucked a blanket around Jill and sat next to her. "You must be frozen, honey. You're shivering."

"I saw a German U-boat!" Jill exclaimed. "Right in Frenchman's Cove! Adrie Dekker and Clayton Bishop met some men from the U-boat and brought them back. I watched from the cliff . . . then Clayton chased me home and I hid on the widow's walk."

"Godfrey!" Quarry exclaimed. "You had them sized up right all along."

"Who knows what he might have done if he caught you," Hugh MacDonald muttered.

"What were you doing out there?" Nana asked.

"I had to find out what was going on, Nana."

"You could have been killed!" Nana exclaimed, hugging her. "Thank God you're all right! This was the first time our meeting went on until after midnight!"

"I'm so glad you weren't here, Nana. He

might have hurt you." Sarge rubbed against Jill's legs, then climbed into her lap, purring.

The sheriff pulled up a chair and patted Jill's hand. "What made you follow them, Jill?" he asked in a kind voice.

"It all began when Sarge here found a carrier pigeon with the message, *Sonnabend iv* attached to its leg. I thought it might be German, but I wasn't sure. Then, when Quarry and I let the pigeon go, it went directly to Clayton Bishop's house. I was suspicious of him because he acted too angry when I happened to stop by and see his pigeons. He was scary! I'd heard about our ships being torpedoed and it made me wonder if some of the shadows we've seen on the sea could have been U-boats. After all, they couldn't very well communicate with Nazi sympathizers. Not with the naval base monitoring radio messages! But pigeons could carry messages from ship to shore with no problem. So when I saw Adrie and Clayton going off into the woods, I followed them. And that's when I saw the U-boat."

The sheriff stood up and motioned to two police officers who stood nearby. "Get over to Bishop's house and see what you can find out. It's probably too late, but I'm going to ring the station and send some men over to the Tearoom Inn. I'm sure Adrie Dekker and the rest of 'em flew the coop hours ago." He went into the hall to use the telephone.

"Locking Jill up there on the roof gave 'em time to get away," Hugh said.

"At least he didn't hurt her." Nana hugged Jill again. "Thank goodness you saw Jill's signal, Quarry."

"I didn't think to look over here right away after I tried to reach you on the telephone," Quarry confessed. "I'm sorry, Jill."

"Clayton Bishop would have gotten to me, if you hadn't called when you did, Quarry. The phone call scared him away," Jill told him gratefully.

"As soon as Quarry saw your SOS, he came straight to me and spilled the beans," Hugh said. "That's when we buzzed the police and got in touch with Elizabeth at Ida's house." He smiled a wry grin. "I'm surprised Quarry could keep a secret this long."

"What about Wendy?" Jill asked the sheriff when he returned. "Where is she?"

"I dunno. We'll know more in a little while. The naval base is sendin' someone right over to talk with you. Meanwhile, we'll wait till we hear what my men have found out. They'll call once they know somethin'." He leaned closer to Jill. "Why didn't you tell anyone about the carrier pigeon or your suspicions, little lady?"

"I heard all kinds of rumors in this town," Jill said. "I didn't know who was sending messages by carrier pigeon or who was receiving them. I was afraid to tell anyone, because I didn't know who . . . might be involved." Jill blinked back tears as she turned to Nana. "I even wondered about you and Tante Ida when I heard her use the word *Sonnabend*."

"No wonder you were confused," Nana said gently, "after seeing the same word in the pigeon's message."

"When you talked to Ida about 'keeping secrets as usual.' I was scared to tell anyone," Jill confessed. "I was afraid you'd get in trouble."

"Well, honey, it's time you knew some of our secrets." Nana squeezed Jill's arm. "It's too bad that we aroused suspicions and gossip, when actually we were trying to do nice things for Winter Haven."

"What do you mean?" Jill asked.

"Our little group gets together to do some good for the community—anonymously. We hear about people who are sick or having babies or new to town, and we try to give them special treats, like flowers, baby clothes, food . . . things like that. We do it anonymously, because—as the scriptures say—'let not thy left hand know what thy right hand doeth.' To get credit or applause for doing good deeds spoils the joy it gives us. Besides, it's fun to let people wonder where the gifts and flowers are coming from."

"The flowers Wendy and I received when we arrived? Were they from *your* group?"

"Of course! And we sent flowers to Adrie when she opened for the season. She didn't seem to have any friends, so we wanted to make her feel like someone cared," Nana explained. "In fact, tonight we packed a basket full of casseroles, baked goods, and flowers that we were going to leave on Guy Binette's doorstep, to show our sympathy for his loss." She sighed. "Not that anything could ever make up for the sacrifice he and Paulie have made."

The telephone rang. Nana answered, then beckoned to the sheriff. "It's for you."

The sheriff talked briefly, gave some orders, then hung up. "Just as I figured, that Dekker woman and her German friends are gone. Looks like she took the girl with her, 'cause there's no sign of any of 'em."

"I should think you could trace them in that fancy car of hers," Nana said.

"Nope. Miss Dekker didn't take the car. It's parked in her garage," the sheriff said. "And Clayton Bishop's car is still in his driveway. Someone else in this town must be involved and helped them get away."

"Perhaps they're heading for Canada," Quarry suggested. "The border's just a few miles from here."

"We've contacted the border patrol, but it's probably too late," said the sheriff. "They may have already passed through."

"Wouldn't they need papers to cross?" Nana asked.

"They've thought of that, I'm sure," the sheriff replied.

Jill spoke up. "Do you suppose they've been taken aboard the submarine?"

"It's poss'ble," Hugh agreed. "Why, they could be halfway 'cross the Atlantic by now."

"Now we know how the Germans communicated with Bishop. He simply brought carrier pigeons to the submarines," the sheriff explained. "When the U-boat wanted to contact him, they surfaced and let the pigeon carry the message home."

"The navy people should be here soon, Jill," the Sheriff said. "And you'd better stay, Quarry. There may be some questions for you, too."

"I ain't goin' nowhere," Quarry said. His father nodded.

Jill watched Quarry's solemn face. The war seemed very close and the enemy very near.

It was after midnight when a navy lieutenant and an investigator from the FBI came to question Jill. "Did you see any number on the U-boat?" the FBI agent asked her.

"Yes. *U-1230*," Jill answered. "I saw it clearly."

"Operation *Elster*," the agent said to the lieutenant. "The first Operation *Elster*, which was to land agents here in Maine on the *U-1229*, failed when that submarine was lost. So they tried again and it worked this time, unfortunately."

"They chose the holiday for their operation, because they knew the whole town would be occupied with its big clambake. No one suspected a U-boat had surfaced at Frenchman's Cove and positioned agents ashore. Looks like they had a lot of help." The sheriff smashed his fist into his hand. "Judas! We had them right here and lost 'em!"

"They were very clever," said the lieutenant. "By the way," he looked at Jill and smiled. "*Elster* means 'magpie' in German."

"They should have named it Operation Pigeon," Quarry muttered.

"Did they all get away?" Jill wondered out loud.

"We were able to locate Max Braun hiding out in a barn near the highway. He was Adrie's cook and entered this country as a Nicaraguan. He speaks perfect Spanish as well as German. He's being questioned now. Bishop and the other two men may be on their way to New York. All the trains heading to Boston and New York are being searched," the FBI agent told her.

"What about Adrie?" Nana asked.

"That woman's been a German agent for several years now. We think she may be under pressure to protect someone over there," the FBI man explained. "The Nazis often threaten the safety of relatives who are still in Germany, and they're able to acquire agents in this way. We're not sure whether she had someone in Germany she was trying to protect or if she was a true German sympathizer. She was being paid lots of money for her work. That's how she could afford that fancy car. She's a clever woman to get away with it for so long."

"But her life ain't worth two cents now that we have proof she's involved in espionage against the United States," the sheriff stated.

The lieutenant nodded. "She could be executed." Jill gasped. "This is wartime, young lady. Think of the number of lives lost off this coast this year. U-boat wolf packs are destroying American ships—many of them innocent merchant ships and fishing trawlers. They don't care who's on board. Adrie Dekker could be to blame for those casualties."

"I feel like some of it is my fault. If only I had told someone earlier." Jill buried her face in her hands and Nana wrapped her arms around her.

"You were temptin' fate, followin' those agents out to Frenchman's Cove." Hugh shook his head. "It'd be time to hang up your boots for sure, if you got caught."

"But she wasn't hurt. And she'll be just fine, thank heavens," Nana said.

"I can't help but worry about Wendy," Jill said. "What will happen to her?"

"We contacted the Taylor family in New York and they're being questioned. We don't think they were any part of this, so Wendy, being a minor, may end up back with them at some point. If we ever find her, that is."

Jill recalled the ruby ring on Wendy's finger. Wendy wouldn't go back to New York willingly, Jill thought. She and Adrie would stay together now—no matter what.

24

When You Wish upon a Star

The blaze-eyed kelpie appeared in Jill's dreams again that night. It gathered itself from the surf and burst into the sky. Galloping in the wind, it soared over the widows' walk and melted into the storm clouds that hovered over the house.

Jill awoke in a cold sweat. The events of the day before came sweeping back. And what about Mom? Why hadn't she heard from her again? The German U-boat was still out there. Dad had yet to take a long trip to New York and the news was full of scares of sabotage to planes. Nothing really had changed. She was more worried than ever!

Jill ached all over and her arm and leg were raw from her fall off the bike. Maybe she'd feel better after breakfast. She trudged downstairs in her pajamas. Nana was in the kitchen, totally absorbed in the radio, which was turned on low. She started when she saw Jill and quickly turned the radio off.

"Hello, sweetheart," she said. "Hungry?"

"What were you listening to, Nana?"

"Er . . . just the news." Nana turned away and poured water into the percolator. Jill noticed her hand was shaking.

"What's wrong?"

"I don't know that anything is wrong." Nana scraped hunks of rationed butter with a knife and plastered it onto bread.

Jill switched the radio on.

"No, Jill," Nana said. "Please don't listen to the radio right now." She tried to turn it off, but Jill had already heard the words "Gulf of Saint Lawrence and the Cabot Strait."

"The Germans have done it again, haven't they? They've torpedoed another boat." Jill turned the volume up loud. "Is it the *Caribou*?"

"I don't know," Nana said. "Sit down, Jill. We'll listen together."

> *"Here's the very latest news on the merchant ship torpedoed this morning near the coast of Newfoundland. We have not been informed what ship it was or how many survivors there are. We do know that U-boats have been finding refuge in harbors along the Maine coast, where they surface at night to recharge their batteries and air the ship. German 'milk cows,' which are older, larger submarines, have rendezvoused with U-boats in our waters, refueling them and bringing supplies.*
>
> *"Nets have been placed in Portland Harbor to prevent U-boats from approaching. However, enemy subs may be hiding out in small harbors and even communicating with German sympathizers. Just this week . . ."*

The news report went on to relate the discovery of the U-boat *1230* in Winter Haven. But now Jill was more concerned about the latest bombing off the coast. Was it the *Caribou*? She turned the knob to another station. "Nana, how can we find out if it was the *Caribou* that went down this morning?" Her voice rose. "I've got to know!"

Nana nodded. "I'll ring up Hugh MacDonald. He can usually find out the news from the coast guard." She took Jill's hand and stroked the little monkeys on her bracelet. "See no evil, hear no evil, speak no evil."

"It doesn't work, Nana," Jill said, her eyes filling up with tears. "I've tried not to see bad things, but they were there anyway. I've tried not to hear evil—but the radio is full of bad news. Just listen to what's happening now!" Her voice broke.

Nana gathered her into her arms. "I know, Jill. You've had so much to deal with in the short time you've been here. I'll ring up Hugh right away and find out what he's heard. You just hold on, honey."

She went into the hall. Jill closed her eyes and waited. Please don't let it be the *Caribou*!

"The coast guard doesn't know yet what ship went down or whether it was British, Canadian, or American," said Nana when she came back.

"We'll have to be calm and wait." She sat at the table and took Jill's hand. "Dear Lord, our Father . . ."

"Don't!" Jill cried, jumping up. "Who does God hear, anyway? Everyone prays—even the Germans! And I'm sure Guy Binette prayed!" The tears streamed down her cheeks.

She ran up the stairs, her bare feet slapping against the cold wooden steps, then raced for the door that led to the widow's walk. Jill scrambled feverishly up the stairs, shoved the hatch with all her might, and thrust herself out onto the deck of the roof. Black storm clouds hovered above the house and the ocean was dark with angry waves, just like in her dream. She thought about the victims out there—the ones who had been torpedoed this morning.

Jill sat cross-legged on the floor and closed her eyes. "Dear God, I'm sorry I ran out when Nana started to pray. I'd rather come up here and talk to you myself, in private.

"You see, I don't understand a lot of things—like this war and people killing each other. I'm so scared that Mom may have been in that boat that went down this morning. I'm scared it may be my fault that the U-boat bombed those ships 'cause I didn't tell anyone about the pigeon and its message. I thought I was doing the right thing. But now, if anything happens to Mom, it'll be all my fault. I never got to say I was sorry for being so mean. Please, *please* take care of her. Please don't let her die. Please."

Jill wasn't sure how long she had been on the widow's walk, when Nana pushed the trapdoor open and poked her head up. Sarge leaped out onto the deck ahead of her.

"I've got good news! Quarry rang to tell us that the ship that was torpedoed was *not* the *Caribou*." As Nana started back down she beckoned to Jill with her finger. "Come on down, Jill. Let's have a cup of tea."

Jill felt like dancing around the roof, but she remembered the victims of the torpedoes—and Paulie Binette and Mr. Wilmar—and all the families that were mourning today, and she restrained herself. She scooped Sarge into her arms and ruffled his fur. "Hear that, Sarge? Mom's okay! She'll be coming back any day now." She looked up at the sky, where bits of blue were beginning to break through the clouds. "Thank you," she whispered.

Later in the afternoon, the telephone rang. Jill ran to answer it.

"Hello, honeybunch!"

"Daddy! Where are you?"

"In New York. I'm singing tonight on *Manhattan Merry-Go-Round*, remember?"

"Daddy, all kinds of scary things have happened up here."

"I talked with Nana late last night and she told me all about it. Oh, Jill, honey, I'm so grateful you're okay. I never dreamed that you'd be in danger in Winter Haven, so far away from the war."

"The war's *not* far away, Daddy. Another ship was torpedoed this morning," Jill said, "but it wasn't the *Caribou*."

"Mom called me last night."

"She did? How did she know where you were?"

Dad chuckled. "Oh, Mom has my schedule memorized! She knew I'd be in New York for the *Merry-Go-Round* tonight."

"Where is she now?"

"Waiting for passage on the next ship. It won't be much longer, Jill. Try not to worry, honey."

"I won't worry anymore once we're all together again. I just wish Mom would get back safely and I wish you'd come up here to Maine too. I wish . . ."

"We'll wish together, okay? Watch for that bright star—you know the one. Then wish with all your might. I'll be wishing too."

"I will, Daddy."

"And listen to the *Merry-Go-Round* tonight. I'll sing a song especially for you."

That night Jill, Quarry, Nana, and Tante Ida gathered around the radio as the theme song urging them to jump on the "Manhattan Merry-Go-Round" burst over the airwaves.

The first song, "I Hear a Rhapsody," was sung by Drew Winters. Jill's eyes filled with tears when she heard her father's beautiful voice.

Dinah Shore sang "Blueberry Hill" and another wartime favorite, "Time Was." Then Jill's dad sang again—"There'll be blue birds over the white cliffs of Dover."

"*Ach!* How I love those words," Tante Ida whispered. "There'll be love and laughter and peace ever after, tomorrow, vhen the vorld is free."

There were other popular songs from Broadway shows, and at the close of the program Jill's father introduced the final song, "When You Wish upon a Star."

"This song is dedicated to my beautiful and brave daughter, Jill. May all your wishes come true, sweetheart."

"Thank you, Daddy," Jill whispered.

25

Tweed

Things were hectic around Winter Haven for the next several days. Practically everyone had their own ideas as to where Adrie Dekker and Wendy were and how they got away. "I had a feeling somethin' was goin' on in that Tearoom Inn," people were saying. "Someone in Winter Haven must have helped those German agents!" No one was beyond suspicion. As Quarry said, "Gossip ain't never been so good!"

On Thursday morning a khaki army truck pulled into Clayton Bishop's yard and Jill went over to see what was happening. Two soldiers were putting the carrier pigeons into baskets.

"What are you doing with the birds?" she asked them.

"They've been drafted by the army," one of the men told her with a grin. "These here birds are right valuable pigeons."

"Now they'll be working for us, instead of the Krauts," the other man added. "They'll carry messages across enemy lines." He tucked a fluttering bird into a basket. "They always fly home — 'cause that's where their mate is."

Jill recognized the brown-and-white pigeon that she had rescued. "Good-bye, little *sonnabend*," she whispered.

On the way back to her house, she was surprised to see Gloria Brandt riding up on her bicycle.

"Hi, Jill," Gloria called. "Wait for me!" She pulled up to Jill and stopped.

"Hi, Gloria," Jill said cautiously.

"I just thought I'd come by to say . . ." Gloria looked down at the ground nervously and kicked at some dust with her sneaker. "Jill, I want you to know I'm sorry the Crystals were so mean to you the other day."

"I don't really care, Gloria." Jill started to walk away, then stopped. "Well, actually, I guess I *do* care. Nobody wants to be treated like that. But the person you were the meanest to was Wendy."

Gloria looked straight into Jill's eyes. "Do you know what they're saying now? They're saying that they were right all along—that Wendy proved she wasn't good enough to be a Crystal—that she's probably a Nazi!"

"I suppose they feel they did the right thing by blackballing her."

"Yes, *they* do. But *I* don't. I don't feel Wendy deserved to be treated that way."

"Then why do you stay on as a Crystal?" Jill asked.

"'Cause I want them to *like* me."

Jill nodded. "It's real important that they like you, huh? Even if they're mean?"

"Maybe someday I'll quit the group."

"Well, good luck," Jill said, walking away.

"When I do, I'll come see you," Gloria called after her. "Okay?"

"Sure," Jill answered, "if *someday* ever comes!"

Back at Nana's house, Jill sat on the back steps

and thought about Wendy and the plans they had made for the summer. Now Wendy and her mother were running for their lives—probably to some foreign country. Would Wendy be scared? Maybe not. Maybe Wendy thinks she's a real spy and enjoying all the excitement. She's probably telling some whopping stories now.

"Jill!" Nana called as she came back from the letter box. "This is for you."

Jill laughed when she saw the scribbling on the envelope: SWAK! VIA TRAIN MAIL! TOP SECRET!

A letter from Patty! Jill ripped it open eagerly.

> Dear Jill:
> SURPRISE! Your grandmother invited me to visit you in Maine! It'll be SO dreamy. Mom says I can come! I'll arrive in Bangor on Sunday at 3 PM! Can't wait! Watch out, Winter Haven! Patty and Jill are together again!
>
> XXXXX Patty

"Nana! Patty's coming! You didn't tell me you invited Patty to visit."

"I wanted to be sure she'd get permission first. I didn't want to disappoint you if she couldn't come."

Jill hugged her grandmother. "You make me so happy! Patty and Quarry and I will have loads of fun." She giggled. "We'll get Patty to look for the fillieloo!"

"Well, now you know why I love secret surprises." Nana put her finger to her lip. "I probably shouldn't say this, but someone else will be coming up on the same train."

"Who?"

"I'm not supposed to tell."

"Daddy?"

Nana just smiled.

Later that day, Jill went up to the widow's walk. The sparkling waters were dotted with brightly colored buoys, marking lobster traps. Jill had come to love this beautiful place, especially now that all the dark secrets had been uncovered. Even the fearful night she was trapped on the roof was just a fading memory. She couldn't wait to share it all with Patty. She and Daddy would be here in two more days!

Jill aimed her binoculars at the Tearoom Inn. It was closed now, the windows shuttered. She looked out at the sea. Was *U-1230* still hiding somewhere out there? Or had it gone back to Europe, carrying Wendy and Adrie with it? She had read reports of German agents who had been transported to Spain by submarine.

A car approached. Jill focused her glasses at a dusty taxi that was rumbling up the road. It turned into Nana's driveway and stopped. The driver opened the trunk and pulled out a suitcase. Jill recognized the baggage.

"Mom!" she screamed.

The back door of the taxi opened and her mother climbed out, looking around to see where the voice was coming from.

"I'm up here on the widow's walk!"

Mom's face lit up with a smile as she saw Jill waving. "Jill!"

Jill slid down the steep steps, then flew down the stairs to the first floor, almost tripping over Sarge. The cat howled and ran under the table, his tail bushing out in excitement. Jill raced through the kitchen and onto the back porch, slamming the door behind her. She leaped off the back steps, dashed down the driveway, and threw herself into her mother's arms.

"Mom!" Jill buried her face in her mother's soft sweater—and the tangy, fresh scent of Tweed.

"I'm home, Jill," Mom whispered. "I'm home."

Afterword

The plot and characters in *Shadows on the Sea* are fictional. However, the mystery is based on recollections from my childhood as well as events that occurred in the real town of Winter Harbor, Maine, during World War II.

I chose 1942 as the year for Jill's adventure because it was the year that a ferry called the *Caribou* was torpedoed. The infiltration of German Intelligence agents into Maine actually occurred in November of 1944. In order to compact the story time-wise, I decided to have the entire plot take place in the summer of 1942.

During this period, the United States and Canada took great care to prevent enemy ships from entering the harbors along the Atlantic Coast. Metal nets were set up in the larger ports, like Portland, Maine. Lights along the coast were dimmed or extinguished; thick draperies covered windows at night; the top halves of automobile headlights were painted black in order to hide coastal cities and towns at night from enemy planes and ships—just as in my story. During that time, children who lived along the Atlantic Seaboard often sat on the rocky shores and watched for periscopes and shadows on the sea.

Despite extreme precautions, enemy ships did infiltrate bays and harbors. Some of these incidents were part of a German plan known as Operation Elster. In English this means "Operation Magpie." The German submarine *U-1229*, which was first commissioned to sneak agents into Maine, was sunk in the Atlantic Ocean by the U.S. Navy. Its mission was then transferred to U-1230. This submarine slipped into the quiet waters near Hancock Point in

Winter Harbor.in November of 1944 and dropped off two spies. It is suspected that the spies who landed in Winter Harbor had assistance from the mainland, but the archives do not indicate who these persons might have been. The two agents were later apprehended.

German officers who were on *U-1230* have since spoken of fishermen's anchors dragging along the hull of their submarine, unaware of its presence. Amazingly, *U-1230* also eluded a U.S. Navy surface search on the way out of the restricted waters. During the day, *U-1230* lay submerged inside the waters of Winter Harbor, only a short distance from the U.S. Navy Radio and Direction Finding Station located on Big Moose Island at the tip of the Schoodic Peninsula.

Did the U-boat officers know this and therefore still its radio communications while close to the Maine shore? I wondered about this, and thought it would be plausible for submarines to use carrier pigeons for the Germans to communicate with the agents or German sympathizers on shore. This is why I created the pigeon *Sonnabend* in my story. I was pleased to recently find records that substantiate this theory.

Carrier pigeons—also called homing pigeons—have been used as message carriers for thousands of years. They were a vital part of the intelligence during World Wars I and II, when they made their way through gunfire, bombings, and storms to bring critical information through enemy lines. Some carried miniature cameras. One pigeon named Scotch Lass accompanied a secret agent into the Netherlands. This bird, though badly wounded, flew back to England with thirty-eight microphotos of German positions and documents. Other pigeons were parachuted into Europe, then carried important information hundreds of miles back to London!

These valiant winged messengers are credited with saving many lives. They were also targets themselves and many were killed or became missing in action. Others, despite injuries, courageously flew hundreds of miles to fulfill their missions. One of the most famous carrier pigeons was GI Joe, who was awarded the Dickin Medal for gallantry by the Lord Mayor of

London. Pigeons received more awards for valor than any other animal! Military pigeons held the rank of captain and were decorated and buried with military honors. Historical records indicate that three thousand soldiers and one hundred and fifty officers were assigned to the U.S. Army Pigeon Service to care for the fifty-five thousand trained pigeons.

There really was a ferry named the *Caribou* that sailed between Cape Breton, Nova Scotia, and Port aux Basques, Newfoundland. It was used during WWII to take military personnel to bases on Newfoundland. At three-thirty A.M. on the calm, dark morning of October 14, 1942, the *Caribou* was spotted by the prowling German submarine *U-69*. A single torpedo struck the *Caribou* amidships on its starboard side, and in less than five minutes the *Caribou* sank into the frigid waters. More than one hundred and thirty-five passengers and crew were killed. One hundred and one survivors clung to debris or huddled in lifeboats. Many of the passengers were members of the American, Canadian, and

British armed forces. Today there is a new ferry named after the *Caribou* that takes passengers to and from Newfoundland along the same route. Aboard the ship one can see a model of the ill-fated earlier ferry and read the story of its brave crew.

In 1942 I was a young child when my mother had to cross the Gulf of Saint Lawrence from North Sydney, Nova Scotia, to be with her dying brother in an outport in Newfoundland. She was a registered nurse and was given special permission to cross through the dangerous waters which swarmed with German U-boats. Although I was younger than Jill, I still recall the fear my dad and I had for Mom's safety. She crossed both ways on the *Caribou*, which was torpedoed shortly after she returned home. A picture of the *Caribou* and her crew hung in our den for many years.

JOAN HIATT HARLOW

is a Boston, Massachusetts, native who now makes her home in Venice, Florida. She is the author of two previous novels, *Joshua's Song* and *Star in the Storm*.